I0690111

Readers love The Elusive Spark series by
ANDREW DEMCAK

A Little Bit Langston

"This was a great, quick read, and lots of fun — exactly what I needed during a long hot summer day and a week of insomnia."

—Queer Sci Fi

"This book started strong, and I was immediately hooked on the mystery of James's powers."

—Love Bytes

Darkfeather

"*Darkfeather* is a delightful read that will leave you hungry for the next installment. Buy it. Read it. Tell everybody about it."

—Skye Allen

By ANDREW DEMCAK

Ghost Songs

THE ELUSIVE SPARK
A Little Bit Langston
Alpha Wave
Darkfeather
Twelve Heroes

Published by HARMONY INK PRESS
www.harmonyinkpress.com

ANDREW DEMCAK

TWELVE HEROES

Harmony Ink

Published by
HARMONY INK PRESS

5032 Capital Circle SW, Suite 2, PMB# 279, Tallahassee, FL 32305-7886 USA
www.harmonyinkpress.com

This is a work of fiction. Names, characters, places, and incidents either are the product of author imagination or are used fictitiously, and any resemblance to actual persons, living or dead, business establishments, events, or locales is entirely coincidental.

Twelve Heroes
© 2022 Andrew Demcak

Cover Art
© 2022 Kris Norris
https://krisnorris.com
coverrequest@krisnorris.com
Cover content is for illustrative purposes only and any person depicted on the cover is a model.

All rights reserved. This book is licensed to the original purchaser only. Duplication or distribution via any means is illegal and a violation of international copyright law, subject to criminal prosecution and upon conviction, fines, and/or imprisonment. Any eBook format cannot be legally loaned or given to others. No part of this book may be reproduced or transmitted in any form or by any means, electronic or mechanical, including photocopying, recording, or by any information storage and retrieval system, without the written permission of the Publisher, except where permitted by law. To request permission and all other inquiries, contact Harmony Ink Press, 5032 Capital Circle SW, Suite 2, PMB# 279, Tallahassee, FL 32305-7886, USA, or publisher@harmonyinkpress.com.

Trade Paperback ISBN: 978-1-64108-289-1
Digital ISBN: 978-1-64108-288-4
Trade Paperback published March 2022
v. 1.0

Printed in the United States of America
∞
This paper meets the requirements of
ANSI/NISO Z39.48-1992 (Permanence of Paper).

For my husband, my hero, Roland,

Clif Snider, *il miglior fabbro*
& Bill Hershon – I miss you both,
N. J., T. G., C. T. R., and S. C.,
my favorite real heroes,
&
S. L. C.
Ei quem primum amavi

"The way to free ourselves is to awaken our heroic potential."
—Carol S. Pearson, *Awakening the Heroes Within*

1.

"ARE YOU all right?" Paul asked.

He squinted down at his best friend, James, lying on his back on the concrete as the late-afternoon sun slanted across his face. Paul shaded his brown eyes with his tan hand.

James shook his head, pushed back his dark curls, and sat up. He rubbed his forehead. He felt a large bump growing beneath his fingertips. 'Oww." James touched the tender spot and felt beads of moisture beginning to form.

I hope that's not blood.

He looked at his hand to be sure—*Nope*—and then up at Paul. "What happened?"

"Don't you remember?" Paul asked with a faint smile. "We were running laps around the school, and I guess you *weaved* when you should have *bobbed*. You hit that pole right there."

James turned his head and saw a metal bar, earthquake retrofitting, stretching horizontally across the narrow alleyway, about head height, between a row of portable classrooms.

"That's a stupid place for a pole."

"Only to someone *stupid* enough to run into it," Paul said with a smirk.

"Ha-ha," James said limply.

Paul reached down and helped James stand up. He was a little wobbly.

"Whoa, there, big fella," Paul said as he steadied his friend. "You were out cold for, like, a minute or two. I couldn't get you to wake up."

"What? You're kidding, right?" James asked, a little bit stunned and now getting a bit frightened. He looked around again. For the first time, James realized something: he didn't know where he was. It looked somehow familiar, but not exactly. He knew he should remember this place, this school, but he didn't. James wasn't sure if he should let on or not. He tried to focus, but his mind was turning, spinning. James knew he had been doing something with Paul, that was for sure, but the rest was hazy. Fear surged up in him like a swirling tide. He felt faint and a bit cold and sweaty. "This is going to sound really weird, but... uh, where are we?"

"What do you mean?" Paul asked quickly. "We're behind the high school. You know, good old Hardwick High. We've only been up here, like, a million times. That must have been some bump you got."

"It must have been," James said and rubbed his forehead again. The sore place throbbed. "Okay, why don't you put your hand on my head and heal me?"

Paul looked at James as if he were speaking in another language. "What?"

"Use your powers," James answered, sounding a little annoyed. "What are you waiting for, Mr. *Blod Heilen*?"

"What are you talking about?" Paul asked and started laughing.

"Heal me the way EBE showed you."

"What?" Paul asked and stopped laughing. "Heal you like who showed me? You're not making any sense."

"Stop playing around, Paul. This thing really hurts. Just do it."

"Do what?" Paul asked again, a little worry now tinting his voice. "You must have a concussion."

"Why are you acting like this? Is it because of your truce with Dr. Albion, or is it about me and Falling Star?"

"Who?" Paul asked and stood back from James. "I think we need to call your mom."

"What? Why would we call her? We haven't even seen her in almost three years. You know it's too dangerous to contact her. We don't know if *Paragon* is listening."

"Para-who?" Paul observed James for a few moments. Paul watched his blue eyes looking back at him, searching him over, and then Paul shook his head. "Maybe you should sit down again. You're starting to scare me. I don't know what you're talking about at all."

James's head ached. *What's happening? Why is Paul acting like this? How can he not know what I'm talking about? What's wrong with him? We're Zetans. We have special powers because of our alien DNA.*

Before James could say or do another thing, Paul reached into his pocket, pulled out his phone, and dialed. "Ms. Kerr, I think you need to come get James. He's hit his head, and now he's acting really strange. What? Okay, I'll call 911. See you soon."

"What did you do that for?" James asked, now a little angry.

"Dude, you're acting totally weird. It would be kind of funny if it wasn't so *serious*," Paul said as he dialed 911. "I bet your mom will be here before the paramedics. You know, it does look like that bump is bleeding a little bit."

James felt the lump on his forehead again. It was pretty big. He felt a tiny drop of wetness. *Blood!* He *was* confused. *Maybe I'm not making sense. Is this a bad dream? Maybe I do have a concussion?* James thought about his power. *That's it. Let me use it right now. Then I'll know I'm not dreaming.* He stretched out his right arm, splayed his fingers, and concentrated. Nothing. He tried again. Still nothing. *What? Where is my electricity? Why can't I shoot out a bolt of lightning? Where are the white sparks?* His mind whirled and whirled and fear again filled him up from the pit of his stomach to the top of his head. *This can't be happening. It's a dream. I do have superpowers. So does Paul. Or he did, didn't he? I'm so confused.* James felt his knees give way as he slumped back down on the ground. Paul rushed over and held him.

"You're okay. Everything is going to be okay. The ambulance is coming right now."

"But what about Lumen and Keira? Where are they?"

"Who? We don't know anyone with those names," Paul said. "You remember me, right? Paul, your buddy. It's summertime. Senior year doesn't start for two and a half months. It's summer vacation. We were going to steal your mom's Tesla and drive up to San Francisco, just the two of us. Remember?"

"I don't know. I don't think so," James said and racked his brain. "Why don't I remember?"

"Umm, you just totally hit your head and were out cold. That might have something to do with it."

"Yeah, but what are all these memories I have that you don't know anything about?"

"Memories?" Paul asked. "You're just saying random things. I can't even understand you."

James shut his eyes and tried to focus again. *I know something has happened to me. I was at the Paragon Academy, wasn't I? Why doesn't Paul remember? I met Lumen there.* James's mind began to wander. He tried to bring it back into focus. *Wait, what's Lumen's last name? Why can't I think of it? And Keira had a little sister? No, a brother. Was that at Paragon or at Fort Bragg? What's going on with me? It's like my memories are draining away. I'm watching them circling my mind. They're disappearing into blackness. Why am I forgetting them?*

The paramedics arrived. James was quickly examined, put on a gurney, and loaded into the back of the ambulance. The two EMTs made sure he was strapped in tightly and closed the ambulance doors. James observed through the back window as Cindy Kerr, his famous artist mother, arrived in her new Tesla.

"Dammit!" she shouted as she looked out the Tesla's open window at Paul. James could hear her voice distinctly even from inside the ambulance.

"I stopped working in my studio and rushed right down here. You'd think in a fast car like this, I'd get here in time to talk to James before they loaded him in there." She huffed a little and then smiled again. "Do you want to come with me to the emergency room?"

"Yeah," James heard Paul say. "I was with him when it happened. Maybe they'll want to ask me some questions."

"Hop in."

James watched Paul run around the Tesla and get in on the passenger side.

"Buckle up for safety," James heard Cindy say, and he laughed to himself about what a careless driver his mother was.

Safety? Yeah, right!

The yellow-and-green emergency vehicle pulled away from the curb on its way down to Little Company of Mary Hospital in Torrance, CA.

Cindy put the pedal to the floor, and chased the ambulance all the way down Hawthorne Blvd. to the hospital.

"MY SON, James Kerr, was just admitted here." James heard his mother through the plastic curtain that separated the examination room, where he waited on a paper-covered table, from the emergency room admitting station. He imagined what the hospital staff were thinking about his mother with her paint-splattered overalls, the gigantic crystal earrings that dangled from her stretched-out earlobes, and the shock of her bright pink hair.

"Who is the attending doctor?" Cindy asked loudly. "I must speak with him *immediately*."

James leaned forward a little on the table so he could see the admitting nurse looking at his mother and then at her computer screen. "Your son is just finishing up with the doctor, Ms. Kerr. You'll be with him in a moment."

"But I must speak with the doctor *now*. I don't want just *anyone* treating my son. Who is this doctor? What are his credentials, hmm?" James's mother slapped her palm down on the counter as she leaned over and glared imperiously at anyone who dared to look back at her.

James saw Paul stand back as the drama unfolded. Paul knew better than to get in the way of Ms. Cindy Kerr when she was on a roll like this.

"Dr. Price is one of our best, and *she* will be speaking with you in just a moment."

Cindy looked down at the nurse and then relaxed a little bit. "Very well," she said, as if calling a truce. "Inform me as soon as the doctor is ready for our consultation. Come with me, Paul." With a snap of her fingers and a wave of her hand, both she and Paul exited for the ER waiting room.

James sat back and waited in silence for the doctor to arrive and examine him. He must have dozed off because in the next moment, James was in a wheelchair being pushed by an orderly, who parked him in the middle of the waiting room. James stood up, still confused, and touched his forehead.

"Your son has had quite a nasty knock," Dr. Price said as she looked over at James and then the notes on her iPad. "Fortunately, it's only a minor concussion."

"Oh, that is good news, Dr. Price," Cindy said, smiling at James and then Paul. "Anything I need to do once he gets home?"

"He's been sedated, and we gave him something for the pain. When that wears off in a few hours, give him ibuprofen and keep a close eye on him. Also, here's a prescription," Dr. Price said as she handed a white piece of paper to Cindy. "It's a little something to help James's brain function come back to normal."

"Come back to *normal*?"

"He's had a serious head trauma. We need to take all precautions to make sure he fully recovers and his memory comes back to normal."

"Memory…?" Cindy began.

"He was saying some really weird things," Paul added from behind James. "I was with him when it happened."

"It's perfectly normal. He's bit confused, but nothing to worry about. As the swelling goes down and the pressure is relieved from his brain, his memory will come back."

"Thank you so much, Dr. Price," Cindy said and shook the doctor's hand.

James moaned and staggered a little.

"Darling!" Cindy said and swooped in to hold him up. "Let's get you home right now. Come on, you two."

Paul smiled at James, who shook himself from his mother's grasp.

James would have smiled back, but he felt so dizzy from the impact and the sedative. "Take me home. I'm very tired right now. I need to rest."

"Your wish is my command."

2.

JAMES OPENED his eyes into the bright afternoon sunlight and rolled over on his bed. His room looked the same as he remembered it: jeans hanging over the back of his desk chair, Antony and the Johnsons poster curling up from its edges on the wall, same patchwork *kakebuton* on his bed, same everything. *Why am I expecting it to be different? It's like I never left. Or did I leave? I don't know anymore.* He got a quick jolt of pain from his forehead; the emergency room medication had worn off. *Ugh, now this! It's weird, but it feels good to be in bed in my room. I feel safe. I'll ask my mother later what's been going on. I guess I needed some rest. It was a nasty bump. I got almost a concussion, the doctor said. I can't understand where all these thoughts, or are they memories, came from. Maybe hitting my head did it. I have quite an imagination, don't I? What other explanation is there?*

James sighed, rolled onto his back, and stared at the ceiling. He pulled the comforter up to his chin and closed his eyes again.

Something small hit James's window. Maybe a pebble. And then something a little larger hit it. He turned to see the clock read 7:15 a.m. *Whoa! I've been asleep since yesterday afternoon! That must be Paul out there trying to get me to wake up.* James pulled back his bedding, walked over, and lifted the blinds. Paul stood right on top of a newly planted purple azalea, now smashed flat, and waved at James. James laughed and opened the window.

"What's up?"

"How are you?" Paul asked as he shifted his weight from one leg to the other and then brushed his black bangs back. "You really had us worried."

"I guess I'm okay," James said and yawned. "I can't believe I slept, like, eighteen hours."

"You needed it," Paul said, laughing. "You were saying the most random things."

"I know," James replied. "But I don't know why."

"Do you still want to go shopping today for our trip?"

"Our trip?" James asked.

"Yeah, we're still going up to San Francisco, aren't we?"

James stared at Paul blankly.

"Come on," Paul said, sounding a little bit flustered. "We finally figured out when it would be a good time to steal your mom's Tesla and go on a road trip and you can't remember that?"

James shook his head. "I don't, really. I'm sorry. It must be the bump."

"My dad already arranged it so we can stay at his buddy's condo up there. We'll have it all to ourselves."

James looked shocked. "Your dad did *what*?"

"He knows we're going to sneak away. He's cool with it."

"Your dad hates me," James said flatly. "He thinks I'm a bad influence on you. Like I'm going to turn you gay or something."

"Too late for that," Paul said and grinned at James. "And he doesn't hate you. What made you think that?"

"Umm, all the times he chased me out of your house and told me not to come back."

"What? You are so *high*! He likes you. He's glad you're my boyfriend."

James recoiled in stunned silence. "He's *glad*?"

"Yeah. At first, he thought I wouldn't be up to your mother's standards, but once they talked about it, everything was fine. You remember, right? We all went out to dinner at Neon Mikado in West Hollywood?"

James put his hand to his forehead and closed his eyes. "I think I need to lie down again."

"Really? But you just woke up."

"Yeah, but my head still hurts."

"Okay, text me later," Paul said and turned to leave but stopped. "We have to go shopping so I can pick out our *vay-cay* wardrobe." He grinned like a madman at James.

"Okay. I'll text you when my head doesn't hurt so much. I just need to lie down again."

"See you."

James closed the window and lowered the blinds. As he walked slowly back to bed, something glittered on his dresser. He wandered across to see what it was. James picked up the silver lapel pin, a dancing satyr encrusted with diamonds.

"Where did *you* come from?" James said aloud. *I thought I lost you at the Shrine Auditorium when I went to the Oscars! I wore you on that fugly Fendi tux Mom made me wear. I've looked all over for you! I can't believe it. My favorite pin returned to me!* He held the jeweled character to his heart and then looked at it again. It was cold and heavy in his palm. James kissed it and then put it away in a small box inside his sock drawer. *There you go. I promise I won't ever lose you again.* He waltzed happily over to his waiting bed, bounced in, and pulled the covers over his head.

"HOW'S YOUR head, my little dumpling?" James's mother asked as he wandered into the kitchen a little before noon.

"It's better, but it hurts," James said as he grabbed a banana from the fruit bowl and began to peel it.

"I'm sure it does," she said and stood up from the table and went to the refrigerator. "Do you want some of my homemade kombucha?"

"Ick! I hate that stuff," James said as he made a sour face and plopped down into a chair. "Isn't it alcoholic, anyway?"

"Only *mildly*," James's mother said, a little sadly.

"Did you find my satyr pin?"

"What?"

"You know, the one you gave me for my birthday."

"Was it missing?" she asked as she removed a jar of fermented green tea and closed the refrigerator door.

"*You know* it was missing. I lost it at the Oscars a couple years ago."

"But darling," his mother replied. "You've never gone to the Oscars with me. You always refused. Something about capitalism ruining modern film—a sentiment that I support completely, by the way."

"Really?" James asked, puzzled.

"I know how stubborn you can be, just like me. I'd never force you to do something you didn't want to do."

"I guess I'm still a little confused. I could have sworn I lost it."

His mother sat and reached her hand across the table to touch James's. She smiled at him soothingly. "You're going to be just fine." She unscrewed the jar of murky liquid and took a quick swig. "Oh, that is so good. Are you sure you don't want any? It really helps loosen your root chakra."

"I'm sure," James said as he caught a whiff of the foul substance and grimaced.

"I know I'm not supposed to know anything at all about your secret San Francisco getaway with Paul coming up," his mother said casually. "But I want you to know it's perfectly okay with me if you want to take the Tesla. You have your license, and we're insured, you know. You can still tell Paul that you stole it, if you want to, if that makes it more fun. But you and I will know the truth."

James didn't know what to say. Sure, this person looked like, and was sort of acting like, his mother, same crazy hair and clothes and odd morals. But something didn't sit right with him. Something was a little bit off. Why wasn't she mad about them wanting to steal her car behind her back, which he guessed had been the plan since he didn't actually remember any of it. *Why isn't she fussing about Paul's family? I know she really doesn't like his father at all. She calls him a vulgarian. It's really weird. I'm glad she's being so much more accommodating. That's a nice change. Or has she always been like this? I mean, she's a famous painter, a true Bohemian. She's always wanted me to be more wild and crazy like she was when she was a teenager. I suppose I'm wild in my own ways.* James's thoughts drifted off again.

"Earth to James," his mother said and waved her paint-smeared hand in front of his face.

James started a bit. "Sorry, my mind just wandered off."

"Apparently, I'm not a very *stimulating* conversation partner."

"You are. It's just my thoughts are playing tricks on me."

"Don't be absurd. You are *perfectly fine*. You've had a head injury, and now you are getting better. End of story."

James rubbed his eyes. He picked up the splayed banana peel in front of him, and without thinking, lobbed it toward the trash can on the other side of the kitchen. It cartwheeled through the air and landed perfectly in the container with a swoosh.

"Three points," his mother said and applauded.

"I don't know why I did that," James said suddenly. "And I can't believe it actually went in. I'm usually so uncoordinated."

Before his mother could answer, James took a paper napkin from the holder, wadded it up, and threw it toward the distant trash can. The paper ball soared through the air and landed right in the bin.

"Very good, James."

"How can I be so accurate from way across the room?"

"You take after me, of course," his mother said, smiling, and looked him up and down. "You've got talent. One of, I'm sure, many hidden talents. But it's not hidden *anymore*. You should try out for Hardwick's basketball team."

James reached down and pulled off his shoe. He threw it, and it landed perfectly inside the trash can.

"I say, you *are* getting good at this."

He pulled off his other shoe and threw it with the same result.

"This is impossible. I should have missed at least once," James said, truly puzzled. "Do you have any coins?"

"What for?"

"I want to try something."

"My Gucci clutch is over there on the counter."

James retrieved his mother's expensive handbag. A black-and-red leather coral snake coiled around the handle. He fished out a quarter from the bottom.

"Heads or tails?"

"Oh, I don't know— Heads."

"I think it's going to be tails."

"Well, we each have a fifty-fifty chance."

"We'll see about that." James flipped the coin into the air. He caught it and slapped it on the back of his left hand. "See? Tails, just like I said."

"You will be right half the time. Those are the odds."

"I don't think so. I bet you the next ten times it will be tails."

"Deal."

James began flipping the silver coin into the air, each time getting the same result—tails. "It's impossible. This whole thing is impossible. It's like I now have permanent good luck or something. I can't even get in trouble with you anymore, and Paul's dad is suddenly nice and not an asshole? It doesn't make any sense." James got up from the table and headed back to his room.

"Where are you going?" his mother called out.

James ignored his mother's question and closed and locked his bedroom door behind him. He walked to his desk and took the silver letter opener from his pen cup. He got down on the floor by the wall outlet. *If I push this in there, nothing should happen. I'll be safe. I won't get electrocuted.* Without hesitating, James guided the metal tool into the open socket. A bright flash of green energy washed over him. He felt nothing, no burn, no shock. James dropped the letter opener and stood up. Not even a burn on his hand. "This place isn't real. I'm not at home. This isn't my room. Paul and my mother aren't real either. This is some kind of *illusion*!" Just as he uttered the last syllable, the word began echoing loudly all around him.

Illusion, illusion, illusion!

Bright lights turned on, blinding him. James felt himself rising, as if floating up from the depths of a deep pool. Up, up, up he went!

JAMES JOLTED awake in the arms of Lumen Kim. He had been lying on a metal examination table, his limbs held inside a soft leather harness. She stared at James as she undid the straps, her brown eyes liquid and penetrating, her long black hair pulled back into her usual ponytail.

"Took you long enough."

"What? What happened?" James asked, rubbing his eyes.

"Give yourself a second," Keira said as she approached the two of them. She wore a form-fitting neon green spacesuit. The color clashed with her bright red hair. "It'll be a minute to remember everything. Just take a few deep breaths."

James looked around him. It was coming back to him now. He was on a spaceship. Not just any ship—his father, Kun's, spaceship. James looked out a portside window and saw the planet Venus close by, its atmosphere swirling, orange and brown. Panels of blinking lights glowed along the walls as ambient energy danced across the ceiling in tiny purple sparks. *I'm on my father's spaceship*, he reminded himself again, as if to make it more real for himself. *We're in space, away from Earth. Paragon thought this ship was the Nibiru object on a course to destroy Earth. But it wasn't. It was Kun coming to rescue us. They got it wrong.*

"But they were still willing to sacrifice us, remember?" Lumen chimed in as she read James's thoughts. "Keira and Alexander touching? Their opposing powers creating a black hole and destroying the Nibiru object and us with it? Project Darkfeather? That was Paragon's plan."

"I remember," James said, rubbing his eyes again with his fists. He touched his forehead briefly and was surprised not to find a bump there.

"You passed the hardest psychological test of them all," Kun announced as he waddled into the room, a look of pride on his inverted-pear-shaped face. He blinked his enormous obsidian-black eyes as he looked down at James. "Congratulations, my son, you discovered the secret of the Hidden Mountain in your subconscious. You are now officially one of the Twelve Heroes."

"I am?" James asked. "That's awesome!" He smiled and looked at the others gathered around him. "That was so weird, but I'm glad I passed."

"We all are," Keira said. "Each of us had to pass through the Hidden Mountain in our minds before Kun knew who could sit in the Circle of Twelve. We're just waiting for the coming syzygy. All twelve of us have to be there for it to activate the amulet."

"I don't remember that part," James said. "The circle of *what*?"

"Of course you don't remember," Lumen said. "No one is told about the Circle until *after* they pass the test. The Circle of Twelve is how we're going to defeat Paragon and release all their prisoners. You know, all those poor people stuck in the Sculpture Garden?"

"How could I forget?" James asked incredulously. "It was horrible. All those people with hundreds of tubes pumping fluids in and out of them while the system drained off their life energy." James shook his head, as if trying to dislodge the memory. "What are we waiting for? Let's free them now."

"The Circle only appears when all the planets in this solar system line up in syzygy," Kun answered. "And that's going to happen very soon. We still have to get the rest of the Star Children on board to see which ones are the Heroes."

"But why can't you save the prisoners yourself? You put a whole army battalion to sleep when we were out in the desert," James reminded Kun. "Remember?"

"That was different. I was using a technology that is now forbidden by the High Council on Hjarta," Kun said and sighed. "You'll see, James. We'll only be able to free all the prisoners with the combined powers of the Twelve Heroes."

"Who's here so far?" James asked as he looked around the large ceramic room.

"You, Lumen, and Keira," Kun began, and then indicated the two young men standing in the corner. "Cedric and Alexander, of course.

That's five. And then there are the Star Children from other parts of the world you haven't met yet: Nga from New Zealand, Tyler from Australia, Troy from Canada, and Stephen from Wales. I have them bunked on another level below us right now. They passed through the Hidden Mountain a little over week ago. They're waiting to find out who the other Heroes are, just like you are. They'll be so glad to meet you all."

"So that's nine total?" James asked. "We still need three more."

"There are *ten* of you that are confirmed Heroes," Kun said as he looked down at a glowing rectangular object in his hand.

"Who's number ten?" Lumen asked and helped James off the exam table.

"That's Philip. You'll meet him soon enough."

Keira looked over at Kun. "I thought only the US Army had access to that top-secret genetic material that made all of us into Star Children."

"They do," Kun replied and put the glowing object beneath his left arm.

"Why are there Heroes from New Zealand and Canada?" Keira asked.

"The US Army still conducted experiments partnering with their ally nations."

"We don't know who the two other Heroes are, do we?" Lumen asked and let her shiny black hair down, pulled it straight, and refastened it. "We have to go back and get Paul, Tenzing, and Falling Star and test them. Right?"

"What?" James asked. "Why Paul?'

"He became a Star Child after he received a Zetan blood transfusion. He may still be a Hero," Kun replied. "And from what you've told me about Tenzing and Falling Star, they may be Heroes too. We won't know until I send them all to the Hidden Mountain."

"I'm so glad I got out of there," James said with a sigh of relief.

"The only way out is to discover that it's an illusion," Lumen said.

"Of course, none of you knew that going in," Kun continued. "It's different for everyone. That's the true test of a Hero: you had to find out it's a tantalizing illusion and reject it. Even if I told you what to expect, the illusion is so powerful, you wouldn't remember anything from beforehand. But you all have passed so far."

"James took the longest," Lumen teased.

He blushed a little bit. *I should have known they would turn this into a contest between the Heroes. Lumen loves a little competition.*

"In my journey to the Hidden Mountain, I went back home with my real mother," Keira said. "We were having a great time, and everything was perfect. That was too good to be true. She was always working for Paragon. I knew it."

"I was with my mother too," Lumen said. "We were at this weird Hollywood party with all these annoying actors and producers. Everyone kept telling me I was going to be a star and wanting to do screen tests with me. Ugh, I hate that life."

"The Hidden Mountain exists within all of us. I had each of you use a Dharma Stone to go into deep meditation to go there," Kun said to James as he reached over and removed the mottled gem in the leather headband that James was still wearing. "You see?"

They all looked at the glittering stone.

"I knew something was wrong in there because everything was going right, like, all the time," James said with a little laugh. "I was super lucky with everything."

"You could have stayed there, you know, if you wanted to," Kun continued, a dark gleam to his huge black eyes. "Mentally, you would have been in permanent bliss, but physically, in a coma-like state until you starved to death."

"Is that what happens to non-Heroes who take the test?" Alexander asked and then glanced out the window as something caught his eye. An asteroid belt shimmered past in front of him. "Do they get trapped in there forever?"

"Sometimes," Kun replied.

"Would you want to go back there, James?" Alexander asked as he looked up at him with swirling white-within-black eyes.

James shook his head. "No, thanks. When everything is just given to you, nothing has any meaning. That's no fun."

"Wow, you sound like a Buddhist monk," Cedric said as he walked over from the glowing console where he'd been standing. He wrapped his arms around Keira's waist and gave her a quick kiss on the cheek. Keira blushed and pushed him away.

"You mean he sounds like Tenzing," Keira said, and then sadness crossed her freckled face. She looked around at her companions, one by one. "We have to go back to Earth, back to Paragon as soon as possible and rescue him."

"And save our favorite yeti prince too," James quickly interjected with a smile.

"Tenzing and Falling Star, yes, both of them," Keira continued. "I can't stand it that we're up here, safe and sound, and they are still down there at the mercy of Dr. Albion and the Paragon Academy."

"And worse, Falling Star and Tenzing don't know we're still alive because they think that Project Darkfeather was successful," James added.

"It's going to be really tough getting back inside there," Lumen said and pulled her long black hair down again, braiding it. "Paragon takes its security seriously."

"But they think we're dead," Keira added. "Paragon definitely aren't *expecting* us. That should help us get in there, right?"

"It's true," Kun said. "On both counts. It's going to be difficult to go back there undetected. But I think we may have the advantage over Paragon because they *do* think you're all dead. That works to our favor."

"But how will we get back inside?" James asked as he took off the last part of the safety harness he'd been wearing and set it on the table. "There are so many guards and cameras."

"Not to mention the psychics they have remote-viewing the entire property, looking for intruders," Lumen said.

"When my ship captured yours...."

"His name is Y'Luc," James said suddenly. "You captured Y'Luc."

"Yes, Y'Luc. You all disappeared from their radar. They assumed their plan worked. They think the Nibiru object was destroyed. They have no idea that the object was my ship the whole time. I cloaked it soon after, so it disappeared too. We are invisible to them. We should be able to fly down to their back door without them suspecting anything."

A flock of Zetan thoughtforms, like living dreams, purple-winged and glowing, breezed through the cabin, dancing above the gathered teenagers and off into the main hallway to find their recipients. Lumen gazed up at them and smiled. She thought she was the only one who could see them. "I wish human thoughts were as lovely as Zetan ones."

"They are," Kun said. "But they rarely travel outside of the human brain."

Lumen laughed.

A reptile-like creature about three feet tall, with greenish-gray scaly skin and sharp quills down its back, entered the room and stopped in front of Kun. Its eyes glowed orange-red, and two fangs protruded from beneath its upper lip. A forked tongue flicked in and out of its mouth, tasting the air.

"You wished to see me?"

"Yes, Philip," Kun began. "I wanted you to meet the other Heroes."

The teenagers turned to look at the strange creature.

"How do you do?" Philip said and gave a little bow, his shiny scales clicking and rippling all over his body.

James looked at Lumen.

Is that a... what do they call them? James thought. *Those things from Mexico that kill goats.*

"Chupacabra?" Philip answered with a giggle.

James stood in embarrassed silence.

"I can read thoughts too, just like you guys."

"Only some of us are that powerful," Lumen answered and raised her left eyebrow.

"I'm sorry," James fumbled. "It's just that I've never met someone like you before."

"It's okay. I get that all the time," Philip said and rubbed his spiny hand over his chest. His claw tips tapped on the octagonal scales. "Goat sucker, Vampire of Moca, Grunch, Peuchin, Sigbin. Terrans have all kinds of names for me. I'm famous on Earth. They even used pictures of me as inspiration for movie monsters," Philip said and paused, smiling. "You ever see *The Dark Crystal*?"

Lumen nodded while the others stood around, blank-faced.

"I was the model for the Skeksis."

James and the others looked at Lumen for an explanation.

"It's a Jim Henson film from the 1980s," Lumen began. "Oh, never mind."

"Where do your people come from?" Cedric asked as he came closer.

"My people?" Philip blinked.

"Aren't there more of you?" Keira asked.

"Oh no. I am the original, a one-of-a-kind *omnimorph*," Philip said and again gave a little bow. "But please, call me Philip."

"Philip has picked up genetic samples of every life form he's come in contact with from all across the galaxy," Kun explained. "That's how he's a Hero. He has Zetan DNA in his system. In fact, he's host to the living cells and DNA of thousands of organisms."

"And I can become any one of them at any time," he said, grinning, his two long canines glistening. "You want to see me turn into a Woji?"

"That's okay, Philip," Kun said as he raised his three-fingered hand into the air. "You'd hardly fit into this room if you did."

"Some other time?" Philip said and winked a bright red eye at Lumen.

"But how'd you get the name Philip?" Cedric asked. "If you are the only one of your kind, who named you?"

The scaly omnimorph turned to Cedric. "I gave myself that name."

"So you must be from Earth, then, because that's a human name," Cedric reasoned.

"I don't know where I came from originally," Philip replied as he lifted a clawed finger and held it to his pointy chin. "I drifted in space for the longest time before I settled down on what you call Earth. The rest of the universe calls it Terra. You are all Terrans. But I *do* consider it my home. I took the name Philip as a remembrance of my friend, Philip II of Macedon, after he died so many years ago."

"Oh," Cedric said, clearly not expecting that answer at all.

"In regard to your earlier request, Keira," Kun began. "I'm going to send you, James, and Lumen to Paragon to collect Tenzing, Falling Star, and Paul. We have to be quick, though, while they aren't expecting us."

"When do you think we'll be going?" Lumen asked as she walked up beside Cedric and took his hand. He squeezed hers back. She looked over to Keira, who smiled at her.

"Right away."

"Like, now?" James asked.

Kun nodded his huge head.

"But I just got back to this reality."

"You're ready," Kun replied. "Your ship, I mean, Y'Luc is fully charged, and so are all of you."

"But we don't know if Falling Star and Tenzing are at Paragon anymore," James said. "Maybe they moved them?"

"And the last time we saw Paul, he was at Project Jedi up at Fort Bragg," Keira added. "That's five hundred miles from Paragon."

"Don't worry, my dears," Kun said as he waddled in front of the teenagers. He took the glowing object from beneath his arm and held it up. A luminous 3D map of the earth appeared. The image zoomed in on Southern California, and then the Paragon Academy. Three red dots blinked on the location. "We've located all three of them at Paragon right now. And we have the element of surprise on our side. Y'Luc has been fitted with a cloaking device so they won't see you coming. He knows where to take you. The only complication is how to get you three back inside of Paragon itself."

"Once we're topside, James and I can open a portal and teleport in," Lumen said, already figuring out the solution.

"That's an excellent idea," Kun said and clapped his spindly hands. "You really are Heroes, aren't you?" He stared proudly at them all. "I can see why Paragon spoke so highly of you all."

James's ears perked up. "When did you speak with Paragon?"

"What? Oh no, dear boy. Not Paragon," Kun said quickly. "Must have been a slip of the tongue. Old brain! I meant the *Pentagon*. We intercept their security transmissions all the time. Did you know that they've classified you as a Type I weapon of mass destruction? They were thrilled that Nibiru was destroyed and you with it. Little do they know!"

James looked at Lumen.

Aliens make mistakes too, you know, James, Lumen thought to him. *Kun hates Paragon. You know that.*

"Well, no time to lose," Kun said and clapped. "Go to your quarters and get your flight suits ready. Meet me in the hangar bay in twenty minutes."

Keira turned to Cedric. "You'll look after Alexander while we're gone, right?"

"No problem," Cedric said with a toothy grin.

Keira smiled, leaned in, and kissed Cedric's cheek.

"You'll be back before he knows it, anyway," Cedric added.

"I'm right here over here, you know," Alexander said. "You don't have to talk about me like I'm not in the room with you."

"Sorry." Keira looked over at her younger brother and was quiet for a moment.

"I'm not afraid, Keira," Alexander said and looked at her.

"But you get so worried when I'm away," Keira said and bit her lower lip. "I want you to know I'm okay and everything is okay."

"I'm safe here," Alexander said, and suddenly transformed into the spitting image of Philip. He rippled his scales and flexed his jaws and fangs. "No one is going to hurt me here."

"That's very good," Philip said, impressed. "You're as handsome as I am."

"He'll be just fine," Cedric said.

"Would you stop worrying?" Lumen said. "Alexander is not in any danger."

"I know. It's just hard now that we're back together. I still think of him as my baby brother."

"That's a good thing," James said. "You should feel protective of him. I want to get down there and see Falling Star. I'm sure he's a mess. For a big, tough yeti, he's such an emotional guy."

"He's a softy!" Lumen snickered. "Like ten-ply soft!"

James shot her a look.

"We could try to send a message to them ahead of time," Keira suggested. "To let them know we're okay."

"It's too risky," Lumen replied. "We don't know if Paragon is monitoring thought-signals. We don't want any of them, especially Dr. Albion, to know about our plans."

"She's right," James added. "Let's get ready and meet up with Kun in the hangar."

"Like Kun said," Lumen added. "We've got no time to lose."

3.

FALLING STAR, the seventeen-year-old yeti prince who was covered with beautiful golden hair, looked over at the tabby cat sleeping soundly on his army bunk. The cat's fur rose and fell with each long, slow breath. Above, rows of fluorescent lights buzzed and lit the dormitory room with a sickeningly pale light. It had been three weeks since the Nibiru object was destroyed and Earth had been saved from its certain destruction. The Paragon Academy was finally getting back to normal.

The yeti leaned forward and put his head in his hands.

At what cost, though? My sweet James died. I know he's a hero and saved the world, but I'll never see him again. The only person I ever truly loved. I just started planning our handfasting ceremony. It was going to be a big surprise. My whole Saesq'ec clan would be invited from Nepal, Myanmar, and everywhere else around the globe. And now he's gone. Gone forever. A tear loosened itself and slid down from the corner of Falling Star's eye.

The tabby stirred and looked over at the golden yeti. "Are you okay?"

Falling Star raised his head and wiped the tear from his hairy cheek. "I don't think I'll ever be okay again."

"I know it's hard. It's only been a few weeks. Give it time," Tenzing said.

"I know. I miss him so much," the yeti said. "I miss them all."

"I do too. Such amazing young people." Tenzing got up and stretched, and then hopped down and walked over to Falling Star's bare feet. "It's all part of the wheel of Samsara, the endless cycle of creation, destruction, and rebirth. We all play our parts." The tabby lowered his head sadly.

"They are in a better place now. Probably in Amitabha's Pure Land, *Sukhavati*, if Green Tara has anything to do with it," Falling Star said. "Wasn't it Green Tara who gave you the sacred ruby that lets people understand each other?"

"The *Talandi Steinn*, yes," Tenzing said. "And understand animals, too, don't forget. Otherwise, we'd not be having this conversation at all."

"I'm glad you let me touch it and keep some of its powers. You are lucky to have received such a gift."

"Yes, she and EBE both gave me gifts," Tenzing, who was a *tulpa*, a guardian spirit, and also a very wise old Buddhist monk now reborn in the form of a tabby cat, said, and then, as if needing to remind himself. "But EBE's gift is one I must keep secret."

"What was that?" Falling Star asked as he looked down at Tenzing.

"Nothing, nothing," Tenzing said quickly and jumped up onto the table next to the yeti prince. "It's strange because I can still feel Keira. We're still psychically attached, even though I know it's impossible. But I'm still connected to her somehow. I know she's gone too. I am no longer her tulpa."

"Maybe it's phantom-limb syndrome, Little Cat."

"I guess so," Tenzing said and paused. "I wish you'd call me Tenzing and not 'Little Cat.' I'm only this cat for now, you know."

"You'll always be Little Cat to me," the yeti said.

"Well, as long as I'm in this body, that is true," Tenzing said and began licking his left shoulder. "But I may not always be."

"I've got to get out of here. This place reminds me too much of James," Falling Star said. "I've got to get back up North to my forest home."

"I'll come with you," Tenzing said with a mouthful of fur as he stopped cleaning himself.

"Okay, but let's leave right away."

"What's the hurry?" Tenzing asked.

"Why not? You want to stay here?" Falling Star asked, indicating the cramped army quarters with his enormous hand.

"No, but shouldn't we make some plans, look at some maps, or something?"

"Who needs maps and plans?" Falling Star said in a loud voice as he thumped his chest with his fist. "I'm a prince of the Imperial Saesq'ec Clan. The woods are mine. I know them better than I know myself."

"You're right, of course," Tenzing said, a little bit embarrassed. "Okay, I'm ready to go whenever you wish to go."

Falling Star stood, yawned, and stretched, and then scooped the cat up in his muscular arms.

"What's this green rock dangling from your collar?"

"Oh that? That's the gift EBE gave me," the tabby answered, and added, "It's nothing, really. Just a trinket. He called it something. What was it? Oh yes, a 'soul keeper.'"

"I've never seen it before," Falling Star said as he lifted the cat toward his face. "Soul keeper, huh? Does it keep your soul?"

"I'm not sure. EBE didn't have enough time to explain it to me the last time I saw him," Tenzing said quickly. "Could you put me down now?"

"Sure," Falling Star replied as he placed the cat back on the floor.

"I'm not surprised you've never seen it. You're seven feet tall. How could you see something way down here beneath my chin?"

"You're right," Falling Star said with a small grin. He went quiet a moment, and then a serious look crossed his face. "Do you think Paragon will try to stop us getting out of here?"

"They promised that we could come and go as we pleased," Tenzing replied. "They haven't tried anything so far."

"That was then, this is now."

"Well, there's only one way to find out," Tenzing said and motioned to the door with his right paw.

Falling Star opened it and went into the hallway with Tenzing slinking along behind him. There was no one else living in this part of the barracks. It had been reserved for use by the Twelve Heroes, and they were all gone now. He walked to the glass front doors of the building, looked left and right for armed guards, and then went out beneath the ceiling of the enormous man-made cavern that housed Paragon. Above them stretched a metal scaffolding that held banks of yellow sodium lights, which created day and night in the subterranean facility. White cubicles and makeshift offices spread around them between dark stalagmites. Canvas tents popped up here and there as well, filled with army officers and scientists. The white structures stood out starkly against the black limestone walls.

Falling Star's feet slapped softly as they made their way through the maze of temporary offices, testing labs, and artificial buildings. They turned left around the base of an old water tower. It was strangely covered with graffiti, as if it had once been at the mercy of a group of teenagers. Now its slogans and images sat mostly unseen in the swallowing darkness.

"We should go up behind the east dorm," Tenzing suggested. "We'll come out near that observation lab and the freight elevator to the surface."

Falling Star picked up the tabby and ran along the back streets of the fantastic complex. Its images flashed past as he ran, repetitions of black and white, shadow and light. They sprinted around the east dorm, crossed to its right side, and arrived at the elevator to the surface.

"They took the lock off the panel. Now anyone can operate it," Falling Star observed as he pressed the button, Up.

"We'll just see what happens," Tenzing said as he looked around for any military personnel coming to intercept them.

Descending numbers flashed on a red screen above the elevator door as it made its way down from the surface to the cave floor. Falling Star noticed Tenzing's nervous trembling and held him tighter. "It's okay. We'll be back up top in a few minutes."

"I hope so."

The silver elevator doors sprung open in front of them. Dr. Elizabeth Albion, her lab coat buttoned all the way up to her chin and her white hair pinned in a neat tight bun, stood in the elevator in front of them. She was accompanied by two armed guards, a few scientists and lab techs, and Paul, James's ex-boyfriend and Falling Star's sworn enemy. Falling Star took three big steps back as Tenzing squirmed in his arms, preparing to jump away.

"Going somewhere, gentlemen?" Dr. Albion asked in a sickly-sweet voice.

"We're going up top," Falling Star said firmly, then added, "to get some fresh air."

"Oh, by all means, do that," Dr. Albion replied. "It's such a nice day today—September's bright blue weather."

"I hear there's a dog park up there you can run around in," Paul said to Falling Star with a smirk.

Falling Star let out a low growl from the back of his throat.

"Now, now, Paul, we don't want to upset our guests," Dr. Albion said. "Guards, forward."

Falling Star smiled thinly at the doctor and then glanced at Paul, who grimaced back at him as he passed. Tenzing relaxed a little bit in Falling Star's arms as the rest of the passengers exited the elevator and the two of them got on board. As the elevator doors closed, Falling Star caught a glimpse of Paul whispering something to Dr. Albion and then looking back at them, a wicked grin on his face.

"That's not good."

"What?" Tenzing asked. "Could you hear what he said?"

"Just a little."

"What was it?" the cat asked nervously.

"He said something about '… it's all going according to *the plan*.'"

Y'LUC HIT Earth's atmosphere at just the right angle—no bumps or choppiness. He felt the intense heat as he smoothly entered the thermosphere, and the friction of the mesosphere, then the sudden coolness as he parted the stratospheric clouds and began his descent onto the Paragon Academy's property.

James lay in the pilot's position on the bridge, his feet in silver stirrups, controlling thrust and braking, and his hands on the two fleshy steering handles. He could feel Y'Luc moving beneath him; it was like riding a huge friendly animal. He stared through the front viewing screen at the swiftly approaching continent emerging through the cloud banks.

"There's North America, and California, right there," James said, pointing.

"Y'Luc is telling me that he's at full glucose level and holding," Lumen said. "DNA replication and chromosome segregation are on track. Cytokinesis is happening." Y'Luc explained everything to her telepathically. "Energy levels are holding steady."

Keira turned in her seat to face James. "We're right on course. Y'Luc knows exactly where we're heading. I'm using $E = 1.2$ for the deflection angle, $D = 116.5f$ on our current trajectory. That will put us right on top of the Paragon Academy." All Zetan objects, including a biomechanical hybrid like Y'Luc, instantly made someone an expert user simply by touching them.

"Great. I'll ease Y'Luc down somewhere in the back of the property near that airplane hangar where they used to house him. They won't be back there now that they think he was destroyed."

"They can't see us anyway with their radar," Keira added.

"Or their eyes," James said and aimed the ship at the slowly growing speck of bright green that was the Paragon Academy. He flew in low across the tops of ancient redwoods, deployed the landing gear, and landed silently in a grassy clearing. Y'Luc came to rest with a whispering swoosh. James stood up and brushed himself off.

"Y'Luc is kind of hairy."

"Tell me about it," Keira said and pulled a long white hair from her space suit.

The three of them laughed. Lights came on all over the ship, and purple energy pulsed along the walls. The hallways contracted and then opened with muscular reflexes.

"What's next?" Keira asked.

"Let's go survey the grounds. Lumen, you can sweep for any psychic activity. Keira and I will go up on top of Y'Luc and look around."

"Roger that," Lumen said and headed down to the landing bay and the ramp that led to the outside. James and Keira followed.

Once they were outside on the grass, Y'Luc unfurled a long fleshy ladder, like a slatted tongue, from his side. It was visible for a few moments, allowing James and Lumen to climb up on top of him.

"Thanks, big guy," James said and patted Y'Luc's side. *Anyone out there?* James thought to Lumen as Keira and he stood on top of the ship and looked down at the academy grounds.

I'm not sensing anyone, Lumen replied telepathically. *That could be because they're all on those psychic blocking meds so I can't read them.*

Or there really could be no one around topside, James thought back.

I think it's safe to approach," Lumen said and then paused. *Wait a second! I'm getting familiar thoughtforms—who is it? They're coming into focus. Oh my God! It's Falling Star and Tenzing!*

What are they doing up here on the surface? James asked.

Who cares—I'm going to let them know we're here, Lumen answered and quickly sent out her telepathic message. *Falling Star! Tenzing! It's Lumen! Can you hear me? We're all alive. We're here at Paragon to rescue you. Meet us at the secret hangar on the back of the property!*

AFTER GETTING out of the freight elevator, Falling Star, clutching Tenzing tightly, strode quickly through the long white hallway that led to the glittering lobby of the Paragon Academy, the phony school that housed the secret underground army testing facility. They passed through the marble lobby and out its fancy oak doors. No one even looked up from the desk as the two went by, as if golden yetis carrying cats were something they saw every day.

"Let's make a run for it," Falling Star said in a hushed voice as they walked through the front doors.

"My thoughts exactly," Tenzing replied as he jumped from Falling Star's grip and broke into a sprint across the parking lot. Then he veered to the right into the heavily forested part of the property. Falling Star followed, his footfalls slapping loudly across the black pavement. They got twenty paces into a grove of redwoods when a familiar voice rang out in their heads.

Lumen? Is that really you?

"I can hear her too!" Tenzing added aloud.

Yes! We'll explain it all to you when you get here. Come quickly. We're going to take you guys back to Kun's ship.

What? Who's Kun? What ship?

I'll explain when you get here. Run!

Is James with you? Falling Star asked and suddenly began weeping.

Yes. He's here and he's just fine, Lumen replied, a little more urgency in her thoughts. *I know what a shock this is, but please don't get emotional right now. Keira's here too. We need you both to hurry.*

"*Mithaee prabhu!*" Falling Star shouted with great joy, his deep voice echoing across the property. He wiped happy tears from his eyes as he ran. Falling Star ducked beneath a low pine bough and headed off to the left to where the secret hangar was, Tenzing hot on his heels. As they rounded an outcropping of ancient granite and entered the grassy clearing between the spruce trees, Falling Star saw something he couldn't believe—James and Keira were floating in the air twenty feet above Lumen.

Oh, my Lord! They're ghosts! he thought quickly. *This is a trick!*

No, we're all alive and well! Lumen thought back. *Our ship's invisible, that's all. James and Keira are standing on top.*

Tenzing rushed past Falling Star and ran along the forest floor as fast as his little legs could carry him. James and Keira climbed down off the invisible Y'Luc. Lumen sprinted toward their two approaching friends. Tenzing leaped into Lumen's arms as Falling Star lifted both of them off the ground and spun them around.

"I've never been so happy to see anyone in my whole life " Falling Star said as his sweet tears began to flow again.

"I thought we lost you!" Tenzing said.

"It's a long story. We'll tell you everything on the way back."

"Hey! It's my turn!" Keira said as she grabbed Tenzing and nuzzled him, then hugged Falling Star tightly.

"James!" Falling Star shouted.

James ran over to Falling Star and jumped up into his great big arms. They embraced and kissed each other wildly, filled with a love that had now deeply rooted in each of them. Neither of them had felt anything so strong for anyone else before. It was nourishing, the way cool water felt running into a thirsty mouth. James understood it with his whole being; Falling Star was the one for him. The Saesq'ec prophesy of their pair-bonding had been true. They completed each other; the circle was unbroken. He promised himself he'd never be away from Falling Star ever again. They continued to stare into each other's eyes, not speaking a single word. Tears were flowing freely down both their cheeks. They had never felt a happiness quite like this before.

Falling Star released James, who turned to pet Tenzing. "I've never even dreamed this could happen," Falling Star said. "You're all alive!"

"We should get on the ship," Keira said. "We have no time to lose."

"But we still have to get Paul," James said. "Don't forget."

"We just saw him get out of the elevator with Dr. Albion down below," Tenzing said.

"Kun *was* right about him being here," Keira replied.

"Yeah, but what *is* he doing here?" Lumen inquired further.

"I don't know," Tenzing said. "Since the Nibiru object was destroyed, it's been very quiet around here. No one talked about anything. And then Paul showed up last week. He and Dr. Albion kept following us around."

"Yeah, Paul is back to his douchebag self again," Falling Star added with a sneer.

A whirring noise pierced the silent forest around them. It got louder.

"What's that sound?" Lumen asked quickly.

The noise echoed across the redwoods and lonely pines and suddenly seemed to be all around them.

"It sounds like a swarm of angry bees," Tenzing answered.

They all looked around the forest clearing, searching for the source of the sound. It seemed to be coming from high above them now, circling around and getting closer.

"I have a bad feeling about this," Keira said. "Let's get back inside the ship."

Before they could get to the entry ramp, a gigantic wasp, about eight feet long, flew down and landed in the middle of the clearing. Its skin was bright yellow with black scaly stripes. Sharp mandibles protruded from its upper jaw. All at once, its antennae retracted into its skull and its diaphanous wings folded inward. The shiny yellow-and-black skin disappeared and was replaced with tan-colored flesh and a Paragon uniform as Paul now stood before them, completely human.

"You weren't going to leave without saying goodbye, were you?" Paul said as he surveyed the small group.

"What the hell!" James said, stunned.

"Yes, it's me. You thought you'd seen the last of me, didn't you?"

"No, we didn't," Falling Star interjected.

"But," James stammered, "what happened to you?"

"Can't you see?" Paul said and threw both hands outward in a flourish. "I was reborn. I am now even more powerful than before."

"How did you become a wasp-man?" James asked and then corrected himself. "I mean, a wasp-person?"

"That nuclear accident up at Fort Bragg did it. My Zetan DNA protected me from the radiation, but it accidentally crossed my chromosomes with a yellowjacket that was flying by."

"It *was* you!" Keira said suddenly, an angry red flush filling her face. Flashes of Paul switching the couplings on the ship, the Sun Stone, causing a dangerous overload, came into her mind. She saw all of Paul's attempts at sabotage. "I knew it! I knew you had something to do with that accident. I could feel it. You sabotaged our ship at Fort Bragg! You could have killed all of us!"

Paul grinned smugly. "All water under the bridge. We're all here now, aren't we? Besides, how did you survive Project Darkfeather, anyway? *That's* what I'd like to know."

"Kun saved us," James said quickly, and then regretted saying it. "I mean, wouldn't you like to know."

"Well, well, so Kun finally showed his face? Took him long enough. I guess the cat's out of the bag, so to speak." Paul looked down at Tenzing. "No offense."

Tenzing pushed his whiskers forward and hissed at Paul.

"Someone's touchy!" Paul said with a dark smile. "Used up any more of your nine lives, Tenzing?"

"Just ignore him," Lumen said and scooped up the tabby cat.

James took a step toward Paul and looked him right in the eye. "Kun sent us here to bring you back."

"What? Why?"

"He needs to test you," Keira said and stood next to Lumen.

"Well, *I'm* not going anywhere," Paul replied.

"Please, don't make me beg you," James began. "We need to take you back to Kun's ship to see if you are still one of the Twelve Heroes."

"Oh, don't start with that again. Twelve Heroes?" Paul glared at James. "That's a lot of bullshit, if I've ever heard it. They just made that up so we'd behave."

"But EBE told us about it," James said, looking a little bit hurt. "Why would he lie to us? He's your father!"

"Half-father—I still have the real human one, you know."

"Please, Paul, come back for a little while and we'll bring you right back here, or wherever you want to go. It's really important or I wouldn't be asking you."

Paul looked at the group before him: the shaggy yeti prince, the orange tabby, Lumen and Keira, his ex-boyfriend James. Something small, an old feeling, stirred in his heart, but he fought it. Paul pushed it deep inside him, along with all the other ones, down into the cold and the dark that now filled his soul. "No, I won't," Paul said, sounding like a spoiled child. He ran his fingers through his jet-black hair and looked again at James.

"Come on, Paul," James pleaded.

Paul was quiet for a moment. "What will you give me if I do this for you?"

"You'll have my thanks," James said. "Isn't that enough?"

"How about a kiss?"

James recoiled at the thought. Though they were intimate once, those days were long over now that Paul worked for their enemies, Dr. Albion and the Paragon Academy. "You've got to be kidding, right?"

"Don't you love me anymore?" Paul asked, feigning innocence. "Why don't *you* come back to Paragon with me?"

"There is no way on Earth I would go back there, especially not *with you*."

"Oh, but you are going to come with me, James. Like it or not," Paul said, a sickening grin on his face. "*Right now!*"

Black antennae and four wings flashed out of Paul's body as he morphed into his giant wasp form. And then he was on top of James, knocking him flat on his back, his sharp stinger pressed firmly into James's side. James thrashed and screamed, and then slipped into unconsciousness. Before the others could react, Paul grabbed James with his six legs and flew up and away, high over the treetops.

"Come back here!" Falling Star yelled and shook his hairy fist up at Paul's tiny form as it disappeared over the pines. "You coward! You bastard!"

"Oh my God!" Keira shrieked.

"What are we going to do?" Tenzing asked.

"Follow them," Lumen said. "Everyone… get inside Y'Luc."

"But James is the pilot," Keira reminded everyone. "Who will fly us?"

"Y'Luc!" Lumen said. "We'll put him on autopilot and tell him to find James. They have a bond. He should be able to find him in no time."

The four of them ran toward the ship. Y'Luc, sensing trouble, made himself visible as the group approached. He started his engines, already knowing what they wanted him to do.

JAMES RUBBED his eyes with the heels of his palms and looked around him. He was sitting inside the mouth of a large sandstone cave, his back against a rough dry wall. James leaned over and gazed out. The cave was two hundred feet above the ground up the side of a sheer cliff face. Red rock was scattered all over the ground below, as if the cave had only recently been bored out.

Where the hell am I? How much time has passed?

A loud humming noise came from somewhere deep inside the cave behind him. He stood up slowly, dizzy from the dose of wasp venom. He felt a sharp pain in his side. *Paul stung me! He motherfucking stung me!* James noticed, too, a strange pain at the back of his neck. It throbbed. He touched it and felt a little swollen lump. *What else did he do to me?* As he lowered his hand, he felt the power-deadening osmium cuffs from Paragon on his wrists. *Great, now I can't zap my way out of this.*

"Thanks, Paul!" James said aloud in frustration.

"You didn't think I'd take some precautions?"

James whirled around to see Paul standing shirtless, rubbing oil on his lacy wings with his muscular arms. They glittered in the pale light from the cave mouth. He began massaging his firm pectoral muscles, running his hand along his well-defined abs that peeked up from the top of his pants. James looked the other away. "I don't want to see you like this," James said.

"You used to like my body, James. Remember all those nights sharing a sleeping bag with me? What's changed? My flesh is pretty much the same, except now I'm better, stronger and faster."

"Haven't you heard? I'm with Falling Star now."

"That chunky mutt?" Paul said as he retracted his wings and pulled on his T-shirt.

"I happen to be in love with him, for your information."

"In love, huh?" Paul said and circled around in front of James. "Isn't that interesting?"

"Why are you doing this to me?"

"Isn't it obvious?" Paul asked as he leaned his face in close enough to kiss James.

James grimaced and turned his head away. "No. I think you're acting crazy."

"I want you back, James," Paul answered firmly, and then paused to listen. "Do you hear that?"

"What? That weird humming sound?"

"Those are my workers. I command billions of them, hornets, mud daubers, and feisty yellowjackets. They'll do anything I ask." Paul reached his hand out to James. "Come and see the palace I've built for us."

"See *what*?"

"The palace."

"Are you kidding?"

"It's our Palace of Love."

"Have you totally lost your mind? I don't love you, Paul."

"Maybe not right now, but you will, James, in time," Paul said distractedly. "Let me show you something."

Paul led James into the darkness that filled the back of the cave. They turned a corner and entered an enormous cavern that was filled up with a pale, organic light. Huge structures rose up from the gloom and into the greenish glow. But it was hard to make out their shapes in the dim light.

"Where is the light coming from?"

"My workers have enslaved billions of fireflies. You know, *lightning bugs*. 'Lightning bug.' Isn't that still your nickname at Paragon? I thought you'd like that little touch."

"Very funny."

After his eyes adjusted to the low light, James gazed in awe at the sheer size of what stood before him. Every square inch of the cave was covered with the delicate folds of papery wasp nests. In the radiant firefly light, the grayish-brown material undulated over the cave walls in frills, in thin ruffles over the floor, and in huge paper fans all the way up to the high ceiling, fifty feet above them. It looked like a massive modern sculpture. Hexagonal cells covered the walls, each one filled with a large white pupa, now the size of a football, squirming at the center. At the very middle of the cave stood what could only be called a palace. Minarets reached up their intricate shapes into a sunless sky along sculpted walls with high arching buttresses. Rows of picture windows opened upon the luminous cave. It reminded James of the Taj Mahal in India. The palace contained many rooms, and every one of them glowed with eerie green firefly light.

"Isn't it beautiful?" Paul asked.

"I'm truly speechless," James said honestly.

"I did this all for you."

"I don't know what to say, Paul. I'm sorry, but I'm just not into you at all anymore."

"I know, but all that is going to change in a few minutes."

"What?" James asked.

Paul stared at him with a wicked grin.

"What is going to change, Paul?"

Paul raised his hands, and at his command a huge cloud of worker wasps swarmed around James in a thunderous black cloud. He flailed his arms and tried to cover his face, but they kept coming at him. As he backed up against the nest-coated cave wall, the wasps began to encase him with their sticky building material. James tried to tear himself free, but there were too many of them daubing him with the gluey substance. He was stuck to the spot. Within a minute he was completely enshrouded, his whole body covered with thick nest-paper, except for his face.

"It's not *what* is going to change, but *who*," Paul said.

"What are you doing to me?" James demanded as he struggled inside his paper prison.

"I wanted you to have a view of our beautiful palace when your transformation begins."

"What transformation?"

"Didn't you notice the lump on the back of your neck?"

Without knowing why, James's stomach suddenly dropped, cold fear flooding his body. The lump on the back of his neck wiggled.

"You remember that documentary we watched about the wasp called the tarantula hawk?"

James said nothing and only glared harder at Paul.

"The one that lays its eggs on a paralyzed tarantula. Then the larva consumes the spider from the inside out? Well, this is sort of the same. I inserted one of my larvae on the top of your spine. But he's not going to eat your flesh. Oh no, nothing like that. He's going to grow along your spinal cord and up into your brain. He'll take over your nervous system, and then change your DNA so you'll become a wasp like me. We will finally be together, as a mated pair. You will finally love me with your perfect insect body and soul, and we'll live in our Palace of Love forever!"

"You're insane!" James screamed. "*Insane!*"

"There's nothing I wouldn't do for my *one true love*," Paul said and paused. "Be patient, James. It will hurt, I'm sure, but the pain will be worth it. True love is always worth it." With that, Paul sent the swarm of wasps back to building the last delicate folds of the paper palace. Then he turned and walked around the corner, heading toward the mouth of the cave, leaving James to transform alone inside his paper cocoon.

"Paul! Come back! Let me go!" James's scream echoed through the cave unanswered. "I promise I'll love you. But don't do this to me! *Paul!*"

The lump on his neck twitched. James could feel a pulse, faint at first but growing stronger by the second. Sweat beaded on his forehead. Then James felt the first pinprick pains as the larva began spreading its tingling nerve-feelers up and down his spine.

"Paul! Come back!" James howled. "Paul!"

LUMEN TOOK her place along the side of Y'Luc's bridge. She pressed the flesh of the ship's controls and mentally linked with him.

We have to find James! Please, Y'Luc, find James!

The ship responded by closing his landing bay and revving his engines. Keira sat across from Lumen with Falling Star and Tenzing in the seat Cedric usually used.

"Are you guys ready?" Lumen asked.

"Yes," Keira answered for them all.

"Y'Luc says he knows where James is. He can feel him. It's about fifty miles from here, due north," Lumen added. "We'll be there in fifteen seconds. Hang on!"

Y'Luc lifted himself into the air above the clearing, blasted up over the redwoods and into the troposphere. Lumen, Keira, Falling Star, and Tenzing gripped their seats and held on, the g-forces pressing them down hard. In what seemed like only a moment, the ship was descending toward a sandstone mountain range. A cave opening appeared in a cliff face halfway up the mountainside as they soared closer.

"Y'Luc says he's in there," Lumen said.

"Yeah, but how do we get there?" Falling Star asked as he looked through the front screen at the cave. "There's no trail leading to the cave."

"We'll have to jump over from Y'Luc," Lumen replied.

"Let's do it," Keira said, standing up. "Have Y'Luc pull up alongside the mountain as close as he can get."

"I'm already on it," Lumen said as she telepathically communicated the request.

The four of them heard the landing bay opening as the ship hovered near the cave mouth. Falling Star put Tenzing down on the floor. "You need to stay here, Little Cat."

"But why?"

"It's too dangerous. You saw Paul sting James. You know he hates you."

"He hates you more," Tenzing shot back.

"You're still staying here."

Tenzing considered this for a moment. "I guess you're right. I'll stay here and keep Y'Luc company."

"Come on, Falling Star," Keira said as she and Lumen passed him on their way to the landing bay.

"I'm coming!"

The two girls stood on the edge of the landing ramp, sizing up the distance between the ship and the cave mouth. It was about a fifteen-foot jump across. Lumen looked at Keira.

"I think we can make it if we get a running start."

Before Keira could reply, Falling Star grabbed both girls, one under each arm, and leapt across the void into the mouth of the cave. He landed safely and put them both down.

"Sorry for that! I know I should have asked before picking you up. James is always bugging me about asking first before I do that."

"No worries," Lumen said.

"I thought it was entirely appropriate in the situation," Keira said and then went silent. Something was moving in the back of the cave.

Paul turned the corner and saw the intruders immediately. He wasted no time morphing into his wasp form. His shiny wings buzzed into action as he jumped into the air and flew viciously straight at Falling Star.

"Look out!" Keira screamed. "It's Paul!"

Paul collided with the yeti and knocked him to the cave floor. He coiled his barbed wasp legs around Falling Star and then raised his stinger high into the air. A drop of fresh venom glittered on the tip.

"The best thing about my sting is I can control the amount of poison I inject—to merely stun or to kill. You can bet I'm going to *kill* you!" Paul hissed in his weird wasp voice.

Falling Star grabbed Paul by the throat and struggled to pull him off. Paul swung his stinger down and caught Falling Star in the stomach. He moaned in agony as the wasp poison flooded his insides, burning and tearing. Paul pumped the venom in as fast as he could while laughing in his strange hornet voice. Falling Star tightened his grip around Paul's throat and began crushing it with all his might.

An orange light radiated around Falling Star as his healing powers turned on, protecting him from the poison. His body forced the wasp venom to flow backward, up into Paul's abdomen. Paul screamed in anguish as the poison flooded back into his venom sac, bursting it open and filling Paul's lower body with searing pain. He writhed, gagged, and then fainted, his wasp head lolling, black tongue hanging out between his two sharp mandibles. Falling Star released him and let him fall unconscious to the floor. The sting site on Falling Star's stomach healed over in a moment. The orange light faded.

"We need to find James!" Lumen said.

"Let me do something first," Keira said as she scooped up a handful of red dirt and let it fall in a thin shaft from her clenched fist. A spray of white sparks snapped around her hand, transforming the dirt into a length of nylon rope.

"Good thinking," Falling Star said as he took the rope from Keira and quickly bound Paul's legs together. "This should hold him while we get James."

"James!" Lumen shouted.

"Where are you?" Keira yelled.

"In here!" James answered from a long way off. "I'm in the back of the cave."

The three of them ran deeper into darkness and turned the corner. They were stunned by the magnificence of the glowing paper palace, and as their eyes adjusted to the ambient firefly light, Falling Star saw James trapped against the far wall.

"There he is!"

He sprinted over and tore the sticky paper from James and lifted him out of the cocoon.

"Help me! Paul planted a wasp larva at the top of my spine. It's going to kill me! You have to remove it."

Falling Star turned James over and pulled down the back of his flight suit. A red lump, which was getting bigger by the second, quivered beneath the skin on James's neck.

"What can we do?" Falling Star asked the others in desperation.

"Let me see it," Keira said as she arrived at James's side. "This is going to hurt, James."

"Just get it out of me!"

"Okay." Keira slid her sharp fingernail under the thin skin above the larva.

"Aggh!" James shouted.

Blood surged up as Keira forced her finger down into the flesh of the wasp larva. She closed her eyes, and white sparks flashed all around the puckering wound. The larva trembled and convulsed as it metamorphosed into blob of human sebum. Keira removed her finger and placed both her hands on either side of the bloody gash. She pressed down with all her might as the giant pimple popped and discharged its foul contents. She cleaned it away and then wiped her hand on the papery wasp nest.

"Ewww! A pimple?" Lumen asked. "You turned it into a pimple?"

"That's all I could think of," Keira said. "I knew it would be harmless."

"Yeah, but super disgusting."

"But it worked like a charm!" Falling Star replied, smiling. He put his huge hand on James's wound. An orange light emanated from his palm and sealed the cut as all the blood evaporated. He turned James over and kissed him gently.

James rubbed the back of his neck and smiled weakly.

"Now you're all better," Falling Star said.

"Thank you!" James replied as he pushed himself away from Falling Star. "Thank you all! Hey, where's Paul?"

"He's out cold in the front of the cave," Lumen said.

"I hope he hasn't woken up and untied himself," Keira said.

"Not a chance," Falling Star said. "I tied him up in constrictor knots, and Paul doesn't have any fingers when he's that big ugly bug anyway. How could he untie himself?"

"We need to get him on board Y'Luc." James reminded everyone.

The four of them ran back to the cave mouth, and to their complete relief, Paul was still there in his wasp form, trussed up and unconscious on the floor.

"What did he want with you anyway?" Falling Star asked.

"Are you sure you want me to tell you?" James asked. "It might make you jealous."

"Oh, was it like that?" Falling Star replied.

"That palace in there, Paul said that he built it *for me*. Well, for the two of us. He said it was our 'Palace of Love.' That larva was going to turn me into a wasp like him."

"He's insane," Keira said.

"Plus, that's a total lie, because everyone, including him, thought James was dead," Lumen said. "He built that palace just for himself."

"You'd think he'd have more sense than that, even being a wasp," Keira added. "That James would figure it out and not believe him."

"That guy never gives up," Falling Star said.

"I think he just hates the idea that you won James's heart," Keira said.

"That's just too bad, isn't it?" Falling Star replied and looked down at the huge wasp.

"Well, Paul did always have good taste," James added with a grin.

"Help me carry him," Keira said as she picked up one of Paul's thorny limbs.

"Oh, please," Falling Star said as he grabbed Paul's bound legs and slung him over his shoulder like a sack of potatoes. "Let's get on board."

"You're going to have to heal him too," Lumen quickly reminded Falling Star. "He's pretty messed up."

"As much as he deserves to suffer, I know you're right. I'll fix him."

"I think all the power made him go mad," James said a little sadly. "He wasn't this evil before."

"No, he was just a self-obsessed asshole before," Lumen chimed in.

"He wasn't that bad."

"Paul was a textbook narcissist," Keira observed. "If you two stood in front of a mirror, he'd only see himself."

"Uh, that's what you *do* in front of a mirror," James said, flustered. "You look at yourself."

"Why are you defending him, anyway?" Lumen asked.

"We used to be best friends."

"That was before he started working with Paragon and became so twisted."

"I still think there was some kindness left in him, somewhere," James said.

Lumen stared at James. "You've got to be kidding."

4.

"WHAT ARE we waiting for, anyway?" Nga asked as the silver ball began to levitate above her blue right hand. "I wish we knew what we were doing next." She moved her other hand up slowly, and the ball circled around it like a moon around a planet. Nga passed the metallic ball between her hands, faster and faster, until it became a shiny blur.

"It's going to happen during the syzygy," Philip said and leaned closer to Nga, who pulled back and glared at him.

"Keep your distance, mate. I'm concentrating." The metallic ball wobbled over Nga's fingers but kept floating.

"We're going to rescue all those prisoners and be Heroes," Philip continued.

"When is the syzygy?" Lumen asked as she turned to look over at Kun.

"In a little over a week," Kun replied.

All the Heroes were assembled on the ship's foredeck. Kun surveyed the group, his huge black eyes reflecting the light from the many instrument panels along the walls. Earlier in the day, James, Falling Star, Keira, Lumen, Cedric, Alexander, and Tenzing had all been in the communal mess hall and eaten their lunches: baked algae protein in a lichen sauce. It was surprisingly tasty. Falling Star ate three enormous portions on a dare from Lumen. A few of the other Heroes were already there. They watched the others, but no one said anything. By some oversight of Kun's, they hadn't even had introductions yet.

"September twenty-third, to be exact," Kun continued. "The first day of the Autumnal Equinox. This will be a very special time when all the planets in this particular solar system will align perfectly and increase the galactic energies. Remember, the Circle of the Twelve will only appear during the syzygy, and you must be ready to take your seats when it does. The planets will only be aligned for a short time, when their energies will be combined. Right then we'll summon the Circle Keeper."

"Circle Keeper?" Cedric asked.

"The Circle of the Twelve is guarded by an ancient Elemental spirit whose essence is locked in this amulet, the Eye of the Keeper." Kun patted the strange bejeweled object that hung around his skinny neck. In its center was a desiccated piece of wadded-up skin attached to a porcelain disc, as big as a hockey puck. It was also covered in concentric circles of glittering emeralds.

"I wondered what that weird shriveled thing was," Lumen said and pointed to the leathery medallion.

Keira replied. "It looks like it died a long time ago."

Kun noticed the girls watching the medallion. "Yes—the Eye is mine to command," Kun replied as he again touched the ancient object. "Only the one who wears the Eye may awaken the Keeper."

"Have you done this before?" Keira asked.

"Not yet," Kun replied and winked at Keira. "I had to wait for all of you to be here, first."

"How will we know which seat is ours?" Nga asked as she stepped forward, keeping her eyes on the levitating ball. "They won't have our names on them, will they?"

A few Heroes laughed.

Nga blushed a bright blue-green, suddenly the center of attention. "I just don't want to mess anything up, you know?" She caught the metal ball as it dropped into her azure palm.

"When you enter the circle, your energy crystal will appear above your seat. You will know it because it will glow your personal color," Kun said as pushed a bright yellow thoughtform into the air. It floated a few moments before zooming off, deep into the ship.

"Our color?" Troy asked as his image flickered like a faulty view screen, and then refocused. He scratched his goatee with his holographic hand. "What color would that be?"

Kun looked at the assembled Heroes. "Don't worry. You will only be attracted to the one crystal that is yours. It will show you your seat."

"Where is the Circle anyway?" Tyler asked in his thick Australian accent. He brushed back his brassy hair with a massive hand. He looked like a circus strongman who had been dipped in molten copper. He'd been one of the last Heroes to arrive at Kun's ship. He and Nga had arrived together in one of Kun's time bubbles; she was from Auckland, New Zealand, and he was from nearby Sydney, Australia.

"The entire stone floor of the Golden Moon Temple where the Circle is has been moved here. It's on Level Two. I had it transported from Hjarta especially for this event. Everything will be ready when the time comes."

"You still haven't told us the plan for dealing with Paragon," Lumen reminded Kun with a note of frustration. "What are we going to do after we take our seats in the Circle?"

"That's a good question," Kun said with a mischievous gleam in his huge dark eyes. "The best question of all." He adjusted the medallion. "Once your energies are combined in the Circle, it will allow someone to become the *Frábær Vera*, a superbeing who has access to all of your powers at once, a being whose strength is twelve to the twelfth exponential greater than each of you individually. All they have to do is open the Eye of the Keeper."

"I wonder who that will be?" Tenzing asked in his sarcastic cat voice. "Hmm, let me see, Kun?"

Kun couldn't understand cat language. "Was that monk saying something?"

"Don't mind him. He's grumpy today," James said. "Someone told us something about that back at Paragon, that we can combine our powers in groups of two or three or four or more, and have additional powers. Twelve times twelve would be the most powerful Hero. Was it UBE who told us that?"

"*UBE*?" Kun said, clearly taken aback. "When did you meet *them*?"

Lumen shot a look at James and Falling Star, and then Keira and Cedric. James instantly remembered that the last time they met with EBE and UBE, they were told not to talk about the encounter with anyone, not even Kun.

"We rescued UBE from the Oak Knoll Army hospital," Keira answered without thinking. "They were calling to me in my dreams, so I went to find them."

"But where are they now?" Kun demanded, strangely almost angry.

"We don't know," James said, a little surprised by Kun's brusqueness. "EBE came and got them. I guess they both went back to Hjarta."

"Interesting," Kun whispered under his breath. A relieved look washed over his pear-shaped face. "I don't want them getting in our way."

"How would UBE, or EBE for that matter, get in our way?" Lumen asked.

"EBE is difficult sometimes."

"He's your brother, right?" Cedric asked.

"He is." Kun paused, at a loss for words for a few moments. "Let's just say that EBE and I don't always see eye to eye on this issue."

"What issue?" Troy asked as he pressed closer to the group.

"What to do about Paragon."

"I think you'd be surprised by what he'd want to do to them," Keira said. "He doesn't like Paragon at all."

"He wants us to leave them alone," Kun replied. "He's made that very clear numerous times. We've been fighting about this since the three of us first came to Earth eighty years ago. I want to release all the prisoners they are holding in all their bases. EBE doesn't think we should interfere."

Lumen again cast a disbelieving look at James and Falling Star, and then Keira and Cedric. Troy noticed the sidelong glances and looked back at Stephen, Nga, and Tyler. Philip hung back, picking his canines with a broken-off spine, seemingly amused by this strange discussion.

"That doesn't sound like the EBE I know," James said.

"My mother has known the Royal Oohd family for years. They are one of our extended clans. Why would EBE and UBE come and visit with us, year after year, if they didn't want to interact with us?" Falling Star asked and stared down at Kun. "It doesn't make sense."

"Oh yes, it does," Kun said. "I've known EBE my whole life. You have only known him a short while. He believes we need to leave other civilizations alone."

"But EBE and UBE—" James started to say as a red light began to flash along the wall panel behind Kun. A high-pitched voice came over a hidden speaker.

"Kun to bridge. Kun to bridge," the robotic voice began.

"Oh, what is it now?" Kun hissed with obvious irritation. "We'll have to continue this conversation later." Kun turned to walk into the glowing hallway, heading for the elevator, but stopped midway and looked back. "I promise you," he said directly to James and Falling Star. "EBE and UBE are not who you think they are. Someday, after we've freed all the political prisoners of Paragon, the US Army, and all the governments around the globe, you'll see. We, all of us, are the freedom fighters. EBE wants everything to stay exactly the same. They wouldn't lift a finger to help anyone."

With that, Kun glanced over at the group and was gone.

Keira turned to Lumen. "Is it just me, or was that really weird?"

"I know, right?" James answered.

"I only met EBE once," Troy said. "But that didn't sound like him to me."

"And Kun didn't answer my question either," Tenzing said as he walked around Keira's legs.

"I think he can't understand animal languages. That's all."

"What's his problem with EBE and UBE?" Lumen asked.

"I can tell you guys don't have brothers and sisters," Nga said as she approached the group, the metal sphere now floating a few inches above her left shoulder. She pulled back her blue hair. It perfectly matched her skin and eyes. "It's just sibling rivalry."

"What do you mean?" Cedric asked.

"Brothers and sisters are always competing with each other."

"I have two younger brothers," Falling Star said. "We're friends now, but it's still weird sometimes."

"Do you have brothers and sisters?" Keira asked Nga.

"Of course," Nga continued. "I have a big family back in New Zealand."

"Do your siblings look like you?" James asked.

"Duh. No," Nga said, her cerulean eyes wide. "They are humans, not hybrids like me."

"I'm an only child," James said.

"I'm *well jell* of you then, mate."

"You're what?"

"*Well jell*—you know, *jealous*," Nga explained. "I'd loved to be the only one, never having to share everything."

"Is that, like, New Zealand speak or something?" James asked.

"I guess it's Kiwi," Nga replied. "Hey, T? Do you say 'well jell'?"

"Yeah. It's Aussie too," Tyler answered and walked over to the group. A spiraling comet passed by the portside window as he approached.

"Wow, this is like some kind of cultural exchange," Keira said, laughing. She stuck out her hand to Tyler. "I'm really bad with names. I'm Keira Darkfeather."

"Yeah, we know who you are," Tyler said as he shook Keira's hand. "You're the ginger that Philip likes so much."

"What?" Philip shouted as he looked up from an instrument panel, his dangerous-looking quills suddenly standing up all along his spine and tail. "Shut up, Tyler!"

Tyler smirked at Philip and continued. "I'm Tyler Cervantes, the tall muscular one with the great hair. As you probably guessed, I'm super strong. In fact, I'm the strongest person on the planet."

"Ah, T, gotta love your humility," Nga said and punched Tyler's copper forearm lightly. "I'm Nga Wellsey."

"Is Nga short for something?" Cedric asked as he stepped closer to Keira, placing his whole body between her and Philip.

"Nah," Nga said and started laughing at the pun she made about how to pronounce her name.

"I'm James, and this is Lumen and Cedric." The teens smiled and acknowledged each other.

"I'm Falling Star," the yeti prince added. "And this little cat is our monk friend, Tenzing."

"Wait, what?" Nga asked. "This cat is a monk?"

"Yeah, he's my tulpa, and he's our little Tibetan monk," Keira added.

"Pleased to meet you," the tabby replied. "Wait a minute. Falling Star, you didn't call me Little Cat."

"Well, I know your name is Tenzing to everyone else. Only I call you Little Cat."

Tenzing felt as if he might blush a little bit beneath his fur and whiskers.

"They can't understand you, Tenzing," James reminded the tabby.

"Oh, where are my manners," Tenzing asked. He closed his eyes and summoned the red jewel from his unconscious. The glowing red stone appeared before them. Falling Star plucked it from the air and handed it to Nga.

"Hold this stone and you'll be able to understand this little cat."

"I thought I was Tenzing now?" the tabby asked, annoyed.

"Not to me," Falling Star said.

"I understood that!" Nga said with some surprise. "When does it wear off?"

"Never," James said. "That's the cool part. You'll always be able to understand other languages, animal, alien, or human, and talk to them too."

"That's awesome," Tyler said as he took the stone from Nga. He held it for a moment and then passed it to Troy and Stephen. Philip didn't need to touch the glowing ruby; he could already understand every language. It had been coded into all the DNA he carried with him.

"Say something else, Tenzing," Troy asked.

"Now that I'm the center of attention, I'm getting shy," the tabby cat said.

"That's amazing. I can't wait to find out what my dog back home thinks about me," Stephen said and scratched his unshaved face.

"You might not like what he has to say!" Lumen said, laughing.

The jewel lifted itself up from Stephen's hand and dissolved into the air. Tenzing's eyes flashed red for a moment and then went back to tabby yellow.

"Let me finish my introductions," Keira said. "I know we're all going to be close friends."

"Okay," Troy said.

"That's my baby brother, Alexander, over there," Keira said and pointed.

"Ugh, I hate it when you call me that," Alexander whined and moved over near the doorway. "I'm your brother, but I'm not a *baby*."

"You know what I mean," Keira said. "I know you're a powerful Hero like all of us, not a baby."

"Which gifts did you get?" Tyler asked Alexander.

"Huh?" Alexander replied with a blank look.

"He means your powers," Cedric explained.

"Yeah, what can you guys do?" Troy asked.

"I'm an alchemist and amplifier," Keira said. She picked up a tablet from the nearby counter and held it aloft. White sparks snapped and popped around it as it morphed into a large bouquet of roses that she handed to Lumen.

"Thank you, m'lady."

"I can change into any form of matter," Cedric said. "And I can read objects and know their history, exactly who's been holding them or around them."

"That's really cool," Philip said.

"I can read minds and push people to do things, so you better be nice to me or I'll have your running naked around the ship," Lumen said with a laugh.

"What's your gift?" Nga asked James.

"I can control energy and manipulate anything that runs on energy."

Tyler's eyes lit up. "Can you get money out of ATMs?"

James nodded.

"He can move money around in bank accounts too," Lumen added. "What can you do?" she asked Stephen, who was hanging back in the shadows behind Falling Star, his tall frame cloaked in darkness.

"I'm a luck magnet."

"You're what?" Cedric asked.

"I can bring luck to whatever I do."

"Like if you're gambling or whatever?" James asked.

"Yeah, but there's a price for it," Stephen said and looked at the others with his deep green eyes.

"What's that?"

"In order to get the good luck, I have to give the bad luck to someone, and I can't control what will happen to them."

"It can be really bad," Nga said. "Someone could get hurt or even killed."

"Wow, that's rough," Cedric said.

"That's okay now," Falling Star interjected. "I'm the Blod Heilun, a healer. If someone gets hurt, I can fix them."

"It doesn't really work with people who were killed," James said. "We had that happen to a soldier we were babysitting."

"Why wouldn't it work?" Falling Star asked.

"I don't know why, but it didn't work for Paul when he had the power."

"But I have it now," Falling Star said. "And I'm stronger than Paul ever was."

"We'll just have to wait and see what you can do," Keira added. "Right, James?"

"I guess so," James replied and squeezed Falling Star's hand.

"I'm a virtual being," Troy said.

The group turned to the faint voice off to their right.

"What does that mean?" Keira asked.

"I can project an artificial reality around anyone, make them think they're somewhere else, with someone else. I'm like a holograph most of the time, but I can also become physical when I want to. It's a matter of focusing my atoms."

"That's kind of like Tenzing," James said and pointed to the cat, who was now asleep next to Keira's feet. "He can inhabit different bodies when he wants, but he's like a ghost normally."

"Where'd Alexander go?" Lumen asked as she looked around. "He was just here."

"That's a good question," Keira replied.

"He's the opposite of his sister," Lumen explained to the group. "He absorbs powers and can create the illusion of being anything—another person, an object, anything. We found out the hard way that if those two use their powers on each other, it can create a black hole and destroy all the surrounding matter."

"That kinda sucks," Nga said.

"Tell me about it," Keira said with a sigh. "Paragon tried to make us do it, but Kun saved the day."

James tugged on Falling Star's arm. The golden yeti leaned down. "I'm going to go check on Paul in the medical ward."

"What? Why?" Falling Star asked, clearly annoyed.

"He's my oldest friend."

"Ugh, that guy is such a douche."

"I just want to make sure he's okay. That's all." James smiled up at Falling Star.

Falling Star sighed. "Okay. Will I see you back at our room before I go to the Hidden Mountain?"

"Is that today?" James asked.

"Yeah, you said you'd be there with me."

"I will. It should only be a few minutes with Paul."

"Okay. But come right back."

"I promise."

With that James ducked out of the Heroes' conversation and headed toward the medical part of the ship, the Healing Center. He still felt so guilty about Falling Star thinking he was dead for the past few weeks. They hadn't had any time to talk about it since they came back from Paragon. James was hoping for a moment to start that awkward conversation. He couldn't imagine how terrible it had been for Falling

Star. James wanted to make it right again between them. He felt like he needed to say something.

"WHAT DO you want?" Paul asked sulkily. He was strapped onto a narrow infirmary bed. Osmium cuffs kept his new powers in check. "Are you going to yell at me?"

"Can't I check up on my oldest friend?"

"You're too funny." Paul lifted his arms and rattled his cuffs.

"That's for your own good. We don't want you hurting anyone," James began. "Or yourself."

"I'm not going to, but of course, why would you even believe me?"

James stared blankly at Paul. He looked so pathetic lying there in bed in his medical gown. But James knew better; Paul couldn't be trusted. "Look, we haven't seen eye to eye for a while now, but can't we try to put that aside and work together for Kun's sake?" James asked and sat on the edge of the bed.

"I guess I owe you an apology?"

"I'm not expecting one," James said quickly. "I know that your new power went to your head, or something like that, and you weren't thinking straight. It made you act totally crazy."

Paul looked at James as if he was about to say something but then changed his mind.

"I know you never meant to hurt me."

"Thanks for saying that," Paul said. "But I don't deserve your kindness. I really don't. I'm ashamed of the way I behaved because of Dr. Albion and Paragon. They can be quite persuasive when they want to be."

"You're not the first person to be poisoned by power."

"But I knew better, and you kept warning me, but I didn't listen. All I could think about was ruling the planet."

"Really? That's what Albion promised you?"

"She makes a very compelling argument," Paul said and shifted against the huge pillow behind him.

"I bet she does. But that's her job." James felt a funny twinge for a moment. Something small and electrical turned itself on nearby. He stopped talking and tried to locate the signal by moving his right hand through the air like a metal detector. A rhythmic pulse suddenly revealed itself from inside Paul's left forearm. "What on earth is that?"

"What's what?"

"That pulse in your arm? What did they put in you?"

"In me?" Paul asked as he pulled his left sleeve back.

James placed his hand lightly on Paul's forearm. He sent a quick jolt of electricity into the flesh, frying the small transistor. Smoke rose from a burnt spot. Paul flinched and opened his mouth to complain, but then his eyes rolled back, and he slipped into unconsciousness.

"Oh my God!" James shouted from Paul's side. He tried to shake Paul awake. "Help! Someone help us!"

A Panjoran med tech rushed into the room, his purple tentacles flailing, and pushed James aside.

"Step aside, human lifeform. I need room to function," the med tech said in a sassy voice.

James stood back and watched the Panjoran feel for Paul's vital signs along his throat and wrists. The tip of one of his tentacles searched into the burnt hole on Paul's arm and removed a small piece of circuitry no bigger than an aspirin. He held it up into the light. "I haven't seen one of these in ages."

"What is it?"

"It's really old Zetan technology. You'd call it a Thought Director. It controls someone's impulses."

"Someone was controlling Paul?"

"Affirmative, human person."

James reached over and took the metallic object and turned it over in his palm. "Is that why he was acting totally crazy?"

"Maybe it was malfunctioning. It is an ancient device. They were never really reliable on you primates." The tech continued to run his other five tentacles over Paul's muscular body. "He's fine. Heartbeat, breathing, all normal. He's just unconscious. What did you do to him?"

"I overloaded his circuits, I guess."

The tech quickly dressed Paul's wound in sterile gauze and tape with two of his sticky tentacles.

Paul suddenly blinked wide-awake and sat up.

"What the hell?" Paul said and pushed the groping med tech off of him, who grunted indignantly at the rebuff.

"Thanks for your help," James said to the tech, who nodded. "Are you okay?"

"What did you do to me?" Paul asked as he rubbed the bandaged spot on his arm.

"If that's all you need, I'm all done here," the med tech said and retreated to another part of the sickbay.

"Thank you," James answered again and turned to Paul. "Paragon implanted something in you."

"What was it?"

"This." James held the Thought Director in front of Paul. "That may explain why you've been acting so weird recently. Paragon was controlling your impulses."

"Is that what Mr. Squid over there told you?"

"Yes, and he probably doesn't want you calling him Mr. Squid."

"Still so touchy, James. You should learn how to relax a little more."

"I *am* relaxed," James said as he felt his whole body tense up.

"I can tell now that that thing isn't in my arm anymore," Paul said as he rubbed the bandage. "So, every time I felt an urge or an impulse to do bad things, it was coming from the implant? That would explain why it felt like I *needed* to do them. Now I can tell my mind has been set loose. It's no longer being controlled."

"You still have a lot of apologizing to do," James said as he put the metal device into a tray by Paul's bed. "It may explain why you did it, but it doesn't help with the consequences of your actions."

"For months, I'd open my mouth to say something, and different words would come out. I'd want to say I'm sorry, and instead I'd say something horrible to you or Lumen. I didn't mean to do those things or behave that way towards you guys. I even like Tenzing. I really do. That thing really manipulated my feelings."

"I wondered how you could have become so mean so quickly. That didn't make any sense," James said as he looked closer at the Thought Director resting on the tray.

"It was the implant," Paul said, staring wide-eyed at James. "You know me better than that. I would never have behaved that way."

James took a long look at Paul. He had been James's best friend forever. And then he was his enemy. *Was it the implant that made him act like that, or something else?*

"Do you remember when they put it in you?" James asked as he rolled the shiny object around the tray.

"You know how it is," Paul said. "They're always drawing blood or testing you for something."

"So you didn't know about it?" James asked.

"Maybe. I think they said it was a tracking device or something. I honestly didn't know what they were doing to me."

"And you don't remember anything weird happening after they put it in?"

"No. Nothing."

"But you lost your power. You stopped being able to heal."

"Do you think that had to do with it?" Paul asked.

"Who knows. But that was a big change in you."

"I wonder why they didn't tag you guys with those?" Paul asked as he again shook the manacles holding him to the bed.

"They probably knew I'd fry it with my energy, Keira's body would change it into some harmless substance, and no tiny circuit could control Lumen's mental abilities."

Paul looked up at James. "Do you believe me now?" Paul asked. "I'm really ashamed of the way I acted towards everyone, but you especially. I was a real asshole. Can you ever forgive me?"

"I forgive you. But Lumen and Falling Star are the most hurt by it. They're going to be hard to convince," James said and paused. "And I wouldn't expect too much from Falling Star. He really hates your guts."

"I'm sorry about that too."

"About Falling Star?"

"I was such a dick. I mean, you broke up with me and everything over it."

"Yeah, I did. And even though now I can understand what was happening, my heart isn't that quick to forget about it. I'm going to need some time."

"I understand," Paul said, a little grin on his face.

"What's so funny?"

"You and that big hairy yeti."

"What about him?"

"It's just so weird to see you two together."

James grimaced at Paul. "You may not believe it, but I really love him, and he loves me."

"You loved me once too."

"I still love you," James said, and then noticed Paul perk up a little bit. "But not in *that* way anymore. We're definitely just friends."

"You'll always be my first love," Paul said sincerely.

"And you're mine."

"No one can take that away from me."

"I'm not trying to take that away…," James said as he began to look a little flustered, a small vein pulsing along his right temple.

"Hey," Paul said, changing the subject. "I didn't tell you what Paragon wanted me to do with my new power."

"I was going to ask you that, bee-person."

"Correction, that's phylum Arthropoda, family Vespidae, genus Vespula, order Hymenoptera," Paul said as he sat up straight in bed.

"What?" James stared down at Paul.

"I'm a yellowjacket wasp, not a bee."

"Whatever!"

"Albion said that my Zetan DNA not only protected me from that radioactive blast back at Fort Bragg, it also spliced my genes with a passing wasp. They wanted me to go on spy missions for them. I could fly in under the radar and sting anyone who fought with me."

James thought about how creepy Paul looked as a yellowjacket and shuddered. "Speaking of good old Dr. Albion," James said, changing the subject again. "Tenzing said the last time he was at Paragon, you said something like 'it's all going according to the plan.' What did you mean by that?"

"That's nothing," Paul said a little sheepishly. "Albion always wanted us to seem two steps ahead of you guys. Whenever we were around you, she always wanted me to say something like that, like we knew what you were going to do next. It's psychological warfare with her."

"So she really has no idea what's going to happen next?"

"Yeah, not really. She just guesses."

"She seems to get it right a lot."

"She is a very good guesser."

"I thought she had a team of mind-readers like Lumen who were mining our thoughts for her."

"Nope," Paul said, shaking his head. "You see how it works? You believed her. Her tricks worked against you guys. She's one smart lady."

"I'm just glad we're going to knock her down a few notches," James said with a smile. "She's really had it coming after all the stuff she's done to us."

"Do you know what Kun's plan is?"

"Not yet, but I know it's some kind of superpower he's going to use against Paragon." James paused and looked at Paul suspiciously. "That's the sort of question I'd expect one of Albion's spies to ask."

"I'm not her spy!" Paul said defensively. "You saw that thing that was in my arm. I'm the victim here."

"It just seems a little convenient that I just now found that circuit in your arm. I should have felt it before. It makes me think that they just put that in there."

"I swear!" Paul shouted. "I didn't know about it."

"We'll see," James said and turned to leave. "For now, Kun is right. You're going to stay cuffed and confined until we're sure about you."

"Do what you have to," Paul said suddenly. "You'll believe me sometime. I know you will."

"Maybe." James turned his back to Paul and headed out of the Healing Center to the turbolift at the end of the dark hallway. He still needed to get Lumen's opinion on Paul. James hadn't quite made up his mind. He wanted to believe Paul, but some small voice inside him told him not to. Lumen would find out. All she had to do was dig into Paul's mind. She'd find out anything he was hiding about Fort Bragg or the rest of his time working for Paragon.

James walked down toward the turbolift. The hall was filled with containers holding strange-looking plants from all over the galaxy. Giant green and red fronds stuck out of metallic pots. Orange flowers that looked like leopard faces, with spotted ears and whiskers, bloomed along the hallway. Kun said they were part of the natural air-filtration system.

Sensing James, the turbolift opened. He entered.

"Blue Level."

On Blue Level, James hurried down to the sleep chamber he shared with Falling Star. James hoped he hadn't spent too much time with Paul. Falling Star could be a very jealous guy. He had so many good points: loyalty, strength, and his rugged handsomeness, but for a royal prince, he had a long streak of insecurity. James was hoping to catch Falling Star before he was sent to the Hidden Mountain.

James rounded the corner and walked straight into their room. Falling Star was stretched out on the levitating bed. His arms and legs were splayed out, making him look like a big hairy *X*. He opened his eyes and looked up as James entered.

"Oh, hey! I was just practicing my Zetan yoga," Falling Star said.

"Yeah?" James replied. "It looked to me like you were practicing Zetan napping. You're getting good at it."

"Well, it does relax me. Maybe I did drift off a little bit."

"We still haven't had a chance to talk about things," James said, changing the subject as he sat down on the bed, causing it to wobble.

"We can talk now," Falling Star said and sat up, folding his legs into a half-lotus position. "If you want."

"I just wanted to say I'm so sorry you had to go through all that at Paragon. Thinking I was dead and that you'd never see me again. I can't imagine how awful that was. You know if there had been any other way of contacting you without alerting Paragon, I'd have done it."

Falling Star turned his focus to James. "I know you would have. It's all right, really."

James gave a little sigh of relief. "But I still feel so *guilty*."

"You don't have to," Falling Star said calmly. "I understand. And you're right. It was hard. If Little Cat wasn't with me to talk to, I don't know what I would have done. If I only had Dr. Albion and Paul around, I'd have gone insane. Tenzing really saved me. But it's all water under the bridge now. No point in dwelling on the past. We're together and everything is fine."

"Then why do I feel like such a creep?"

"Is it because of Paul?" Falling Star asked, clearly very curious. "What did you two talk about when you went to see him?"

James was taken aback by the question, even though he had anticipated this kind of scrutiny from Falling Star. The yeti prince never went to bed and slept on an argument in his life. If something was wrong, he wanted to fix it. Now.

"Nothing really. He's doing better. It was weird. I found this implant in his arm that supposedly was controlling his mind."

"That's convenient," Falling Star said with a smug smirk, his mustache curling up at the ends.

"I know, right? That's what I thought." James reached over and took Falling Star's golden hand. He stared at the yeti, carefully choosing his words. "I'm not going to lie to you. Paul did say he wanted me back, but I told him that you and I are together, that we're in love, and he better get used to it. I don't have anything but bad feelings towards Paul. With all the double-crossing he did for Paragon, he went from friend to asshole in under two seconds flat."

"I knew he'd try something like that," Falling Star said, suddenly angry, his eyes looking more like a wild animal's, a little bloodshot around the edges. "He doesn't respect boundaries. In fact, he doesn't respect me!"

"It's okay. Don't worry about him."

"I *do* worry. He stole you away once," Falling Star said and pulled a stray strand of hair from his face. "What makes you think he won't try to do it again?"

James looked at Falling Star. "First, he's chained to a bed in the Healing Center, and second, I told him that I think he's a total jerk."

"That didn't stop him before."

"Listen, he's not a problem anymore. The med tech removed the device that was controlling him. It was some kind of Paragon trick. He's not going to bother us."

"I think that's just a convenient excuse for him being such a dickhead."

"It might be," James said. "But he's chained up in there. I'm in here with you. I'm not going back to see him. I don't *want* to."

Falling Star was silent for a moment, and then broke into a charming smile, dagger-sharp canines and all. He reached over and pulled James into a crushing hug. James laughed as Falling Star ran his fingers up and down James's sides, tickling him. They rolled around on the bed for a few moments, then started kissing. Falling Star was very careful not to put all his weight onto James. He knew it could crush him. They came to rest with James straddling Falling Star's chest like a cowboy in a saddle.

"You're the best thing that's happened to me," Falling Star said.

"I feel the same."

"I want to be with you always."

"Me too," James said with a little laugh. "I can't stand it when we're apart, even for a few minutes. We've lost so much time already."

Falling Star brushed the brown curls from James's forehead and stared into his crystal-blue eyes. "I want us to have a handfasting ceremony when we get back home to Earth."

"Handfasting?"

"Yes, *hand-fasting*," Falling Star said the word slowly, sounding it out.

"You mean, like, get *married*? That kind of handfasting?" James asked, his eyes wide with astonishment.

"Yes," Falling Star answered. "James Kerr, will you *marry* me?"

James's mind did a little cartwheel and then a back flip. "Wait a minute. Will you say that again? I don't think I heard you correctly. Maybe it's something to do with the altitude...."

Falling Star grinned and said, "Will you?" He pointed to James. "Marry me?" And he pointed his golden finger toward himself.

James didn't need to wait with his replay, "Oh yes! Yes! You bet I will. I love you so much!"

Falling Star pulled James down into a crushing yeti hug again. He wiggled free and sat staring down at the teenage yeti. Falling Star looked so handsome—his mustache perking up at the ends, his beard perfectly groomed, his golden eyes sparkling with happiness.

"I never thought I'd get a marriage proposal from a real prince."

"Well, now you have."

"Especially not a *yeti* prince," James said with a grin. "Wait until my mother hears this. It'll knock her socks off."

"Does she have trouble keeping her socks on?"

James glanced at Falling Star and then started laughing. "No. It's just an expression. You know, she'll be surprised."

"Oh, okay. I was going to suggest she might want to put rubber bands around her ankles before you tell her the good news."

"She should probably do that anyway."

"Then it's settled. When we are back on Earth, I'll talk to my mother, and she'll arrange it with our clan High Priestess, Dayaaluta. We'll have a handfasting ceremony to cement our union." Falling Star hugged James again and wouldn't let go. "My mother loves to arrange these ceremonies."

"Queen Chaandani, right?" James asked as he again wiggled free of Falling Star's grasp.

"Yes, that's my mother. We'll have everyone in our forest kingdom there."

"And don't forget Kun, EBE, and UBE."

"They'll be there too, don't worry. My mother is very thorough with her invitations."

"And all the Heroes," James said as he counted out their names on his fingers.

Falling Star watched James and snickered. "I'm sure she won't forget anyone, believe me. She is thorough."

"Does that mean I'll be a prince too?"

"No, you'll be the royal concubine," Falling Star said and crossed his arms behind his head and lay back.

James stared silently down at Falling Star.

Falling Star noticed that James's wasn't laughing, so he sat up quickly. "I'm kidding! I'm kidding! Yes, you'll be a prince too. I promise."

James sighed in relief. "Do I still have to call your mother 'Your Highness'?"

"I still call her that!" Falling Star said and laughed. "That's her title."

"But let's keep our handfasting a secret from everyone for now," James said. "They'll make a big deal of it, and we need to focus our energies."

"Very sensible."

"We're here to save the prisoners of Paragon, and everyone else they've caged up all over the world. I don't want to distract anyone from our mission."

"You tell me when we should share the happy news, and I will."

"Okay," James said as he got up off the levitating bed and offered his hand to Falling Star. "Come on, big boy. Let's send you off to the Hidden Mountain."

5.

"JUST PUT your head back and you'll soon be there," Kun said as he secured the leather strap across Falling Star's forehead. "I have to make sure the Dharma Stone is in position for maximum meditative effect."

The yeti prince grunted and wiggled beneath the protective harness that spread over his huge body. "I wish I wasn't tangled up in this," he said.

"It's for your safety," James answered for Kun. "You'll probably thrash around a little bit. We all had to wear one of those when we went in. We don't want you to fall off the table and hurt yourself."

"Or fall onto someone else and hurt *them*," Philip said under his breath as he lurked in the background, observing the whole process.

Falling Star's ears perked up as he heard the little slight.

"And Falling Star is using the largest harness we had," Kun added.

James stood beside the examination table and held Falling Star's hand. He saw the look of concern on his golden face. "You'll be fine."

"I know," Falling Star replied. "When do I go under?"

"How about right now?" Kun asked. He waved his three-fingered hand over Falling Star's face, activating the Dharma Stone. The yeti's expression changed from tight fear to loose, placid sleep. James let go of Falling Star's hand.

"Now we wait," Kun said and glanced over at James.

"I wish I knew what was going on in there."

"Ask Lumen to show you," Kun suggested with a smile. "That's what we did when you were in there."

"Great idea," James said. "Let me contact her." He closed his eyes and concentrated. *Lumen, are you there? Meet me in room twenty-three of the Healing Center. Falling Star has just gone to the Hidden Mountain.*

Okay, I'm down the hall. I'll be right there, came her quick telepathic answer.

"I'll leave you to it, then," Kun said and shuffled out of the ceramic room on his spindly legs.

Falling Star moaned and shook his head in the harness. James watched with some amount of worry. *What if he doesn't figure it out? What if he's trapped in there by the illusion?*

"He'll be fine," Lumen said, reading James's thoughts as she entered.

"I know. It's just he's such a sensitive guy. I worry about him," James said and looked down at his silver space boots. Then he looked up at Lumen. "I almost forgot to tell you. I found out that Paragon was controlling Paul with this weird device in his forearm. That's what made him turn so evil."

"A device in his forearm? What? That doesn't make sense. We'd have known about it, right?" Lumen asked, her brown eyes fixed on James. "You would have picked up its electric pulse."

"I guess I should have, but I didn't. Even Paul didn't know."

"I don't believe it for a minute," Lumen said and pulled her black ponytail back over her shoulder. "That's just another one of Paragon's lies."

"What if they did it up at Fort Bragg? We hardly saw him there. That could be why we didn't find it," James said.

"Maybe, but I still don't trust him."

"You should go see if you can find out something from picking through his thoughts."

"If I have time," Lumen said. "I do have many other things more important to do than dealing with *Paul*."

"Well, that way we'd know for sure."

"Maybe, but right now let's see what Falling Star is getting up to," Lumen said and placed her right hand onto Falling Star's muscular shoulder. "Grab my hand so I can share this."

James took Lumen's left hand, and suddenly he was going down, down, down into the bottomless darkness with Falling Star.

THE FIRST thing Falling Star saw when he looked up from where he lay in the snowbank was a shaft of light filtering down through a fissure in the ice cave's ceiling. He couldn't remember what had happened before. He was just here, now, in the frigid cold at the bottom of a cave made entirely of ice. The frozen walls shone pale blue all around him.

The light was eerie.

Did I slip through that crack and end up down here?

He couldn't remember.

Maybe the fall affected my memory?

The yeti prince activated his healing powers, just in case something had broken from the three-hundred-foot drop between the ceiling and the cave floor. Orange light engulfed his whole body, filling it with a warm tingling feeling. The cave walls reflected orange all around. The glow slowly faded. Falling Star looked down at his legs, but something wasn't right. He stood, brushed off the snow, and looked himself over.

Why do my legs look so short? And my hands! They're so small!

He felt his face.

Where is my beard? It's like I am a child again. But I'm seventeen. Why do I feel like a ten-year-old?

Wind whistled across the fissure in the ceiling, making Falling Star look up.

What's happening? Where am I?

Falling Star heard voices coming through the crack in the ice ceiling. It sounded like children laughing. A familiar dark brown, hairy face suddenly popped into view across the ice fissure. It was Falling Star's youngest brother, Rishi. But something looked wrong about him too; he was too young.

He should be fourteen years old, but he looks like seven.

"Hello!" Falling Star called up at him.

"I told you he wouldn't be able to make it out," Rishi said as he turned his head back and laughed.

Falling Star's younger brother Anil appeared alongside of Rishi and laughed down at Falling Star. He, too, looked to be about eight or nine years old, not sixteen like he should be.

"You're never going to be the king!" Anil shouted down through the crack.

"Yeah! Papaji always said you were a sissy boy!" Rishi added with a mean grin.

"A sissy boy, always reading!" Anil yelled. "What good is reading to you now?"

"What are you guys talking about? Help me!" Falling Star again yelled up at his two mischievous brothers. His voice came back as a hollow echo as Rishi and Anil both ran off laughing. "Don't go! Get me out of here! This isn't the Royal Initiation!"

Suddenly it dawned on him. Maybe this *was* the Royal Initiation! But he had already gone through that when he was ten years old. Hadn't he? That was the age when a firstborn child of the Saesq'ec Royal Family proved his or her worthiness to be the ruler. It had been a different task, though. Falling Star didn't have to climb out of a slippery ice cave; he just had to bring ten tree trunks down the Kali Gandaki River and build a temple inside the gorge.

Didn't I already pass the initiation and become the heir to the throne? Why do I remember doing it? Was it all a dream?

Falling Star looked around the cave as his eyes quickly adjusted to the low light level.

"What good has reading done for me, huh?" Falling Star said aloud. "I'll show you."

He searched the snow-covered floor for sharp objects, anything, a piece of wood, a broken rock. Falling Star located a thick branch and promptly broke it into two pieces.

"I can use these as pitons," he said again out loud. "I read about ice climbing in a book, *for your information*!"

Falling Star stabbed the sharp end of the branch in his right hand into the wall of ice. It stuck firmly. He pulled down on it, testing his weight against its hold. It wouldn't budge. In went the branch in his left hand, a few feet up. He pulled himself up, removed the right branch, and swung his arm up, stabbing it into the cave wall above him. He repeated the same motions with the branch in his left hand: removing it, swinging his arm up, and stabbing the branch into the ice. Again and again, he did it until he was about halfway up the cave wall, hanging high above the snowy floor. Falling Star pulled out the branch in his right hand and swung it up, and this time it bounced off the limestone that was thinly concealed beneath the ice. His mind reeled for a moment; then he stuck the branch into the ice at the same level as his other hand and hung there.

I'll have to move over and find where the ice is thicker.

Falling Star now swung his body side to side, shimmying across the ice wall, trying to locate a thicker patch that would lead him up to the fissure in the ceiling. After twenty-five feet, he found the spot. The branches stuck in and held. He climbed higher and higher toward the beam of light coming through the crack in the ice. As he reached up, he got a handhold on the mouth of the fissure. Falling Star reached his right hand out and steadied his grip on the ledge with his elbow. He felt the cold wind blowing past his body. His legs dangled above the three-hundred-foot drop. He didn't look down. Falling Star felt weightless for a moment and then pulled himself out of the crack and stood up.

A loud celebratory cheer followed by a shower of fragrant marigold blossoms greeted Falling Star. He looked around him. His whole family, along with most of the neighbors, stood clapping and cheering for him on top of the Hari Parbat glacier. Falling Star's mother, Queen Chaandani, threw her brindled arms wide open and rushed to hug her son. She stood eight feet tall and was covered with black-and-white mottled fur. She wore a crown of ruby rhododendron flowers and a double strand of conch shells around her neck.

"I'm so proud of you, my sweet *Jaanu*! I knew you'd pass the initiation!"

She kissed him repeatedly around his golden cheeks and forehead.

"Mamaji! Stop it," Falling Star said, blushing. "You're embarrassing me."

"What? A mother cannot be proud of her son, the next king of her clan?"

"That's *not* what I'm saying," Falling Star said while trying to disengage from his mother's crushing embrace.

"You've made us all very proud." A deep voice came from behind him.

Falling Star turned to see his father, King Bijalee. The king stood eight-and-a-half feet tall. His shiny fur was dark brown with a graying sagittal crest on top of his head and a silver band of hair on his back that ran across his broad shoulders. He wore a golden crown on his head and two wreaths of marigolds around his neck. He was smiling at his son while his kind eyes twinkled.

"Papaji?" Falling Star asked as tears began to fill his eyes. "This can't be happening. You're dead."

"What?" the king asked. "But as you can see, I am standing here before you. Very much alive."

"It's not possible." Falling Star said as he wiped away his tears.

"But it is," King Bijalee continued. "Now we need to fit you for your crown."

"This is all happening too fast. I can't believe what I'm seeing. You're not really here. This is a trick. It's some kind of illusion, *illusion, illusion*...." The word rang out all around Falling Star as he was blinded by the bright light coming down on him from above. He bolted awake to see James and Lumen by his side.

"You did it!" James shouted and tried unsuccessfully to hug Falling Star through all the dangling safety harnesses. "I knew you would."

"You're a Hero!" Lumen added.

"I am?" Falling Star asked and rubbed his eyes, feeling the dampness of tears on his bearded cheeks.

"Welcome to the Twelve Heroes!" James again shouted and gave Falling Star's hand a squeeze, the only part of him James could reach. "We need to tell Kun."

"No need," Kun addressed the room as he reentered. "I'm here. Very well done, Falling Star. Welcome to our little family."

"Thank you," Falling Star replied to Kun.

"I didn't think you'd have too much of a problem with the Hidden Mountain, Falling Star," Kun began.

"Why is that?" James asked.

"Because the Hidden Mountain is another name for what the Tibetan Buddhists call the bardo."

"Bardo?" James asked. "Is that a place?"

"It's not a place. It's more a *process*. It takes forty-nine days to complete. But basically you are challenged by all sorts of illusions and you need your meditative skills to pass through it."

"But the bardo is something you do after you die," Falling Star added, suddenly realizing how dangerous the Hidden Mountain was. "Are you saying that you've been sending us to the brink of life and death?"

"Aren't we always on the brink? No one knows when they will be called off this mortal coil," Kun said smoothly. "Anyway, we were here monitoring you. If something happened, we'd pull you out."

"I don't like doing dangerous things I know nothing about," Falling Star said. "You should have told us first."

"It wouldn't have made a difference once you went under," Kun said. "And besides, you really were in no danger at any time."

"Plus, you, out of all of us," James replied directly to Falling Star, "would be safe because of your healing power."

"Maybe."

"I always knew you'd turn out to be a Hero like me," James said.

"Now we need to test Tenzing," Lumen said, as if crossing him off a mental to-do list. "We only need one more Hero and then there will be twelve."

"We need to test Paul, too, right?" James asked.

"What? Oh, that's right."

"He's still a possible hero," James reminded Lumen.

"You can do that yourself," Lumen said with a sour look. "He's all yours."

"Oh, come on, Lumen," James replied. "I told you he had some kind of behavioral control implanted in him."

"Implant or not, I don't want to be around him. I don't even want to look in his mind to see if he's lying," Lumen said. "I already *know* he is lying."

"I don't want to be around him either," Falling Star grunted with a look of disdain. "And I don't want you around him, James. He can't be trusted."

"I *told* you, I won't go near him again," James said a little forcefully, his blue eyes widening. "He's been nothing but a total jerk to me. You know that."

"I'll run the test on Paul," Kun said. "You three won't have to be involved. You can test Tenzing."

"Thanks," James said with a sigh of relief. "We'll do that."

"I really hope it's Tenzing and not Paul," Lumen said as she helped Falling Star out of the harness and onto the floor.

"Me too," Falling Star answered.

"ARE *ALL* these straps really necessary?" Tenzing asked as he fidgeted his cat body in the leather harness.

"I asked the same thing," Falling Star said. "And yes, *Little Cat*, they are."

The headband that held the Dharma Stone had been modified to fit Tenzing's small forehead. Lumen laughed when she saw how ridiculous Tenzing looked wrapped up in the tawny leather straps like an elaborate gift.

"Now, there'll be none of that," Tenzing said, starting to get cross. "I don't like being laughed at."

"I'm sorry," Lumen apologized. "It's hard to see you beneath all those harnesses and straps."

"And my name is *Tenzing*, not Little Cat," Tenzing reminded Falling Star for the one hundredth time.

"Do you want to do the honors?" James asked Lumen. "Remember, wave your right hand while thinking of the intention."

"Duh, I was there too, James. I know how this works."

"Yeah, James," Falling Star teased and poked James in the ribs. "You can stop your man-splainin'."

He flinched and then smiled up at Falling Star. "Stop it!"

"Get a room, you two," Lumen said as she waved her right hand over Tenzing, sending him deep into a meditative trance.

"Let's see what's happening," James said as he motioned toward Tenzing.

"Cool your jets," Lumen said. "He just went under."

Lumen reached through the tangle of straps and touched Tenzing on the shoulder and then reached for James's hand. He then grabbed Falling Star's golden fingers.

Blackness.

Blackness and silence.

"Nothing," Lumen said, with surprise.

"This isn't right," James said. "Let's bring him out."

"Give it a few moments," Lumen said cautiously.

"Something's wrong! Bring him out, Lumen."

"Okay," Lumen said as she removed the leather headband from Tenzing and used her own consciousness to lift him back into reality.

The tabby squirmed and looked up, wide-eyed, at Lumen, James, and then Falling Star.

"What happened?"

"Something went wrong," James said. "You didn't go to the Hidden Mountain."

"You were in this endless blackness," Lumen added.

"Well, that settles it," Tenzing said. "I'm not the last Hero. It must be Paul."

"That's just *dandy*," Lumen said, grimacing.

"I was afraid of that," Falling Star said.

"But he still has to make it back from the Hidden Mountain. Don't forget about that," James added.

"Well, at least I'll be able to watch all of you when the Circle opens," Tenzing said. "That should be spectacular. I'm very excited to see that."

"I'm sorry, Tenzing," James said.

"What for? I'm just the same as I was before. There's nothing to be sorry about."

PAUL WATCHED as Kun entered the room in the Healing Center where he was manacled to the hospital bed. He wasn't expecting any visitors, so Kun's presence came as a complete surprise. They'd only just met as it was; Kun was Paul's half-uncle, on EBE's side of the family.

"Don't tell me, let me guess. You're here to see if I'm one of the Twelve Heroes, right?"

"Yes, Paul, that is correct," Kun said as he approached the bed and laid out the leather harness and the Dharma Stone.

"What's all that junk?"

"That 'junk' is going to determine the rest of your life, young human," Kun said with an air of superiority. "We'll know soon enough if you're a Hero or just a parasite."

"Parasite?"

"What would you call someone who does nothing and sponges off of tax-payer dollars?"

Paul stared at Kun. He didn't know what to say in response. "Wow, you really hate Paragon, don't you?"

"No, not Paragon. They are neither here nor there," Kun said as she started to untangle the leather harness.

"You hate us, the Star Children?" Paul asked.

"No, I love my children," Kun replied, nonplussed. "I'm talking about those who refuse to pull their weight. The ones who want everything handed to them."

"You mean me, don't you?"

"Bingo!"

"But I'm not a freeloader! I did everything Paragon told me to do, and more," Paul said quickly. "And all those bad things I did, I couldn't help myself. I was being controlled. Just tell me what you need done and I'll do it. I promise."

"Well, not to worry, Paul," Kun said soothingly. "I'm sure you are a Hero and not a parasite. But there is only one way to find out. Here, slip this over your body." Kun handed Paul the harness.

Paul complied as best he could, working around his manacled wrists, quickly wrapping the leather straps around his torso. Kun finished tightening the harness and slipped the Dharma Stone onto Paul's forehead.

"What's going to happen to me on the Hidden Mountain?" Paul asked, a little fear in his voice.

"If you are good and pure of heart," Kun said, "nothing. You'll come out the other side the same as when you went in."

"And if I'm not pure of heart?"

"That's another story completely," Kun said with a grin and passed his hand over Paul's face. "Sleep now!"

Paul's eyes rolled back into his head and he sunk back into his overstuffed pillow. He could feel the bed break away under him as he started to fall and fall.

PAUL WAS sitting at a fancy dinner table at the Paragon Academy. Dr. Albion was seated to his right and Asmodeus to his left. The table was set with sparking flatware, floral arrangements, and fancy dishes and goblets. There were six chairs but only four place settings.

"When is James getting here?" Dr. Albion leaned over and asked Paul. "Is he running late?"

"I'm not sure," Paul answered quickly, trying to get his bearings.

"He'll miss the main course if he doesn't get here soon," Asmodeus said as he used a clawed finger to remove something from one of his long canines.

"I'm sure he's on his way," Paul said and looked around the dining room. Polished oak panels lined the walls. Portraits of Paragon's ex-directors stared from gilded frames. A bright chandelier hung from the corbeled ceiling. He had no idea which part of Paragon this was, likely a part he'd never been to before. Maybe a place just for its upper levels of staff.

A loud buzzing sound quickly hushed and was replaced by the sound of boots walking along a hallway. James stepped into the dining room, his wings folding into his back slits and his black mandibles retracting all the way.

"Sorry I'm late. I had a little trouble subduing that Italian minister," James said as he took a seat next to Dr. Albion and wiped his sweaty brow. The sweat had turned his bangs into delicate ringlets. "You'd think two doses of my wasp venom would have silenced him! Those Italians have some sort of immunity!"

"Maybe it's from all that awful pasta they eat!" Dr. Albion said, laughing.

"Yeah, all those carbs!" James replied and joined in the laughter. "Well, he'll be at his target weight in about a week, once his body has sufficiently decomposed."

Asmodeus, Dr. Albion, and James all laughed uproariously.

Paul sat staring at James. It was as if he'd never seen him before, as if he were a stranger.

"Yes, Paul?" James asked as he noticed the long stare. "Did I forget something?"

Paul shook his head.

"Oh, of course I did, you silly!" James said as he stood up and walked to Paul's side. "Our after-work kiss."

Paul instinctively puckered up as he had so many times before.

James pulled back.

"Ewww, not like that. Not like some common primate. I want a real wasp kiss." James's mandibles sprang out of his facial orifice and dripped their lubricating slime.

Paul had to turn away momentarily not to throw up. The thought of putting his mouth anywhere near that dripping hole in James's face was almost too much for him. He steadied himself and turned to look at the gaping mandibles. Paul's own mandibles came out, James leaned in, and they gnawed gruesomely at each other, slime dripping between their slippery jaws.

"That's better," James said as he pulled in his mandibles and his mouth returned to its normal size.

A side door opened, and a robot-like person, half metal and half flesh, pushed a cart with four covered dishes on it. The robot stopped next to James and placed a covered plate in front of him.

"Oh, goody! I haven't missed that main course," James said, applauding. "Thank you, Baltimore."

The robot nodded and pushed the cart next to Dr. Albion and served her. Baltimore lifted another covered dish and placed it in front of Paul, and pushed the cart next to Asmodeus to serve him.

"Bon appetit, everyone," Dr. Albion said as she reached over and removed the lid from her dinner.

James and Asmodeus lifted their lids as well, revealing what was beneath.

Lumen's severed head stared up as Dr. Albion maneuvered a fork in and removed Lumen's left eye.

Keira's head sat on James's plate and Cedric's on Asmodeus's.

"Aren't you eating tonight?" James asked as he noticed Paul not lifting the lid on his plate. "You're really going to like your dinner. I had it made especially for you."

As if in a terrible dream, Paul lifted the lid to reveal Tenzing's cooked body, charred and curled on a bed of lettuce. He gagged and slammed the lid back down.

"Oh, come on, Paul. You've always hated that cat," Dr. Albion said as she removed Lumen's other eye and swallowed it.

"This isn't happening!" Paul said as he stood up, pushing his chair backward. It fell to the floor with a loud bang. "This isn't really happening to me! It some sort of terrible illusion! Illusion! Illusion! Illusion!" The word rang out as Paul felt himself lifting off the floor and rising through the ceiling and up into the black sky above.

KEIRA GIGGLED while sitting on Cedric's knee on the real marble bench in the Nature Pod section of Kun's ship. An artificial waterfall rippled down the wall behind them and emptied into a large pond, where multicolored digital carp swam according to an algorithm. A cool manufactured breeze shifted across the illusion of grassy hills and shook the perfect emerald leaves on the symmetrical eucalyptus trees. Lumen heard Keira's laugh echoing along the hallway before she saw her with Cedric. Lumen walked over the soft loam to the bench.

"I was looking for you guys," Lumen began. "I thought we were going to do some more zero-G practice."

"Was that today?" Keira asked as she removed Cedric's hand from her thigh, shifted off his knee, and sat down next to him. "I've lost all track of time here. Mostly because of him!"

"One hundred percent true," Cedric replied. "I don't even know what day it is anymore either."

Lumen stared at them silently for a few awkward moments. "Yeah, it felt a little like you were ghosting me. And now I find you in here, gigging and doing whatever."

"I didn't mean to ghost you," Keira said quickly. "I'm serious. I really have lost track of time in here."

"You've been in a Paragon facility," Lumen said to Cedric. "You know what it's like not to have day or night."

"Yeah, but it's different on this ship."

"Not that different."

"Well, we're all together now," Keira said brightly and ran the zipper down the front of her green space suit. "Who wants to go skinny-dipping?"

"I think I'll pass," Lumen said.

"Oh, come on," Keira pleaded. "Don't be mad at us. We were going to come look for you."

"Really?" Lumen looked at Keira, trying to read her thoughts.

Cedric noticed what was happening and sent a cold blast of fog at Lumen, breaking her connection.

"Very adult, Cedric," Lumen gasped as she waved the swirling fog away from her face.

"You said you wouldn't do that to us," Cedric said.

"Yeah, no spying!" Keira said, standing up.

"I just wanted to know the truth, but I guess I already know you guys have moved on without me."

"No, we haven't," Keira said as she approached Lumen. "Come on, let's go swimming." She tried to grab Lumen's hand, but she jerked it away.

"I'd say you two look pretty cozy together," Lumen said as she stepped away from Keira.

"So that's what this is about?" Cedric asked as he stood up from the bench. "You're jealous of Keira and me?"

"I didn't say I was jealous."

"You're acting like you're jealous," Cedric said and walked next to Keira.

"I'm not."

"Yes, you kind of are," Keira said.

"This always happens with threesomes," Cedric said, sounding very wise. "Someone always gets jealous and controlling."

"When have you *ever* had another threesome?" Lumen asked as she stared at Cedric.

"You don't know what I did after I left Paragon."

"I can find out," Lumen said and fixed her mind on Cedric's thoughts, beginning to sift through them.

"Stop it," Keira said as she pulled a small cloth from her green space suit, threw it in the air, and turned it into a fluttering confetti shower over Lumen, distracting her from reading Cedric's mind.

Lumen slapped at the paper scraps falling on her head and shoulders. She let out a frustrated sigh. Keira stepped back and held Cedric's hand, waiting for what Lumen would do next. As the last pieces of rainbow-colored paper flitted to the ground, Lumen shook her head and walked quickly out into the hallway without looking back even once.

NGA WAS bored. She was stacking chairs on top of one another in a pyramid shape with her mind as Lumen stormed into the dining hall. Lumen stopped in her tracks as the last chair spun through the air and took its place on top of the assembled shape, forming the pyramid's tip. Nga was wearing the same color of space suit that Keira wore, bright green, but wore it with her sleeves rolled up. The color made her blue skin seem bluer.

"Sorry, I didn't know anyone would be in here. I'll leave you alone."

"No worries," Nga said and smiled, turning her full attention to Lumen. "I wouldn't mind a bit of company. Especially female company. Too much testosterone on this ship!"

Lumen laughed. "It's a crisis, isn't it? Too many males?"

"That's very *observant*," Nga returned while raising her left eyebrow. "But really it's too many *horny* males."

"It's kind of gross too," Lumen said. "You're Nga, right?"

"Yeah, and you're Lumen, the brainiac telepath."

Lumen nodded at the blue-skinned girl.

"I've been getting a little antsy in here," Nga said as she guided a chair out of the middle of the pyramid like pulling out a piece from a Jenga tower. It settled in front of Lumen, and she walked over and sat in it.

"Neat trick," Lumen said.

"Thanks. Here's another." Nga waved her right hand and the pyramid collapsed. But before a single chair hit the ground, they floated noiselessly around the room a few inches off the floor and tucked themselves silently beneath the long dining tables.

"That's handy. Must make cleaning up after a party a snap."

"Ahh, my partying days are long over," Nga said and pulled out a chair and sat in it across from Lumen. "That's actually why I'm so antsy. I haven't had a drink in, like, three weeks."

"Aren't you a little young to be drinking?' Lumen asked innocently. *Nga looks to be seventeen or so. Maybe eighteen. Hard to tell with Star Children.*

"Aren't you a little too old to be so naïve?" Nga asked.

"Sorry I asked," Lumen said and got up to leave.

"No, please don't go," Nga responded quickly as she stood and reached for Lumen's arm. "I'm just a little on edge right now. Paragon still has full control of my family, and I don't know what they're going to do to them. On top of that, I could really use a drink."

"I can fix that," Lumen said.

"What? You haven't got a flask on you, have you?"

"Better than that." Lumen looked Nga right in the eye. "You want to quit drinking?"

"More than anything. It's ruining my life."

"Okay," Lumen said and stood close to Nga. "Sit back down on that chair."

Nga complied. Lumen put her hands onto Nga's azure temples and then closed her eyes.

"What are you doing?" Nga said with a jolt as she tried to lean away from Lumen's grasp.

"This won't work unless you sit still and don't move."

"But I can feel you moving things around in my mind."

"I'm just giving you a little motivation to stop drinking." Lumen said, smiling. "This won't hurt a bit, and it will work as long as you want it to. Trust me."

Nga looked up at Lumen.

"All right. You wouldn't be the first person who tried to fix me," Nga said with a note of skepticism in her voice. "My ex-girlfriend tried to get me to quit, but she failed."

"I won't fail."

"Okay, but if you fry my brain, I'm going to come for you."

"Don't worry," Lumen said. "This is perfectly safe. Now let me finish."

Nga sat still and leaned in toward Lumen.

"There we go. You're all done."

Nga blinked up at Lumen. "But I still feel like I need a drink," Nga said and searched Lumen's expression for an explanation.

"Whenever you feel like drinking, just imagine the color blue and you won't want to drink."

"Blue, huh?" Nga asked and glanced down at her blue forearm and then up at Lumen.

"I figured it would be easy to remember," Lumen said with a cheeky grin as she sat back down across from Nga. "Try it."

Nga closed her eyes and then opened them, a look of pure surprise on her face. "It's gone! The desire to drink is gone!" She reached over and grabbed Lumen in a huge bear hug, then released her. "Sorry! I have no boundaries!"

"No problem. I could see in your mind what a tough time you've had. Of course you'd try to dull your pain in some way. That's completely reasonable," Lumen said and then paused. "But the effect isn't permanent, I'm afraid. The only way to stay sober is to join a support group, like Alcoholics Anonymous."

"What? Why is that?"

"It's only *a suggestion* I put in your head. For it to become a permanent part of your hardwiring, you have to keep it up with meetings and stuff."

"That seems easy enough."

"Yeah, my mom is in AA," Lumen said. "I shouldn't be breaking her anonymity, but you are part of all that now. Everyone in Hollywood is in AA or NA or some other twelve-step program. It will make your life easier. It really will."

"Yeah, mate. It wasn't easy being the only little blue kid in town, believe me. The doctors thought there wasn't enough oxygen getting to my skin, but as soon as my powers started manifesting, it was clear that was not the reason. That's when they sent me away from New Zealand to the Paragon Academy in Sydney."

"It must have been hard for you," Lumen said sympathetically.

"Yeah, there were so many fake friends before I went to Paragon too. 'I don't see your color.' How could you not? This color defines my whole experience. I don't want people to take that away from me. My life matters."

"Yeah, being Korean around some white people can be like that too," Lumen said and pulled her long hair over her left shoulder, examined the tips, and then tossed it back. "Those are the people I call liberal bigots."

"Yeah?"

"Like if I'm on a plane, some person will sit next to me and ask if I'm Chinese. When I say Korean, they start telling me about how much they love Korean food or how they love 'your people.' Gah! It's so annoying! I'm like, hello, I'm American."

"One of the things I liked about Paragon…," Nga said and stopped, hearing how ridiculous it sounded.

Lumen made a sour face.

Nga continued, "… and there isn't that much to like, really, there isn't."

Lumen seemed satisfied with that answer and grinned back at Nga.

"The thing I liked was being around so many people like me. I wasn't the weirdo anymore."

"Yeah, I get that," Lumen said. "And Paragon totally used it against us."

"I know, right?"

"I met James at Paragon in Los Angeles."

"And he's with that Bigfoot guy."

"Falling Star is a yeti."

"Oh, sorry," Nga said, catching herself. "Is it offensive to say Bigfoot?"

"I don't think so. It's just he identifies as a yeti. I respect however people want to identify themselves. You know, whatever pronouns they use, etcetera."

"Too right." A look of relief passed across Nga face. "You know, they call them Yowies in Australia."

"Really? I didn't know that," Lumen continued. "But there's more. Falling Star is a prince."

"Wow," Nga said. "He does have really beautiful hair. I'm not surprised he's royalty."

"James and I became fast friends at Paragon. It's funny, too, because we both have famous mothers."

"Really? That's cool. What's your mom do?" Nga asked as she adjusted the collar on her suit.

"She's an actress. You ever see *Starship Galaxian*?"

"Wait! No way! I freaking love that show! Your mom is Andromeda, that cyborg, right?"

"Yep. That's her."

"Oh my God! I knew it. That is so cool. I can't wait to tell Tyler. He loves that show too!" Nga smiled at Lumen. "So you're, like, totally famous, right?"

"I hate all that Hollywood stuff."

"What's to hate? The fame, the fortune, and the limos? The champagne wishes and caviar dreams?" Nga said in her best imitation of an American accent.

Lumen laughed at how silly Nga sounded. "Everyone is totally fake. They just use you to move their careers forward. It sucks. It really does."

"It can't be all that bad," Nga said and unconsciously leaned a little closer to Lumen.

"Here," Lumen said and took Nga's hand. "I'm going to show you a memory. This should cure you of ever thinking that the Hollywood life is glamorous."

"Okay," Nga said and looked Lumen in the eye. She noticed that they were topaz with flecks of orangish amber, like gemstones. *So beautiful.*

"My mom dragged me to one of the typical 'networking' parties they have in Hollywood when I was much younger. It was held at a huge house up in Laurel Canyon that used to belong to Harry Houdini."

"Who?"

"You know, that magician. The one who could bust out of handcuffs and chains."

Nga shook her head.

"He's from the early 1900s."

"Nope. Sorry, mate."

"Anyway, it was at this big Hollywood house with a swimming pool, walk-in wine cellar, and an elevator, blah, blah, blah. My mom thought I would have some kind of acting career, so she arranged for

me to meet this famous agent who represented child actors at the party."
Lumen's brown eyes widened, and she then squeezed Nga's hand.

NGA WAS walking along a dimly lit Spanish-tiled hallway. Behind her
she could hear the sound of people laughing; a loud party was in full
swing. A man in a dark suit walked ahead of her. Through a long window
she saw a fountain running with glittering water, spotlights shining on it.
The sky was dark and clear, full of stars. She could see all the pale lights
of the houses that lined the canyon beyond.

"Your mother says you show a lot of promise," the man in the suit
said. "Let's go to one of the back bedrooms where it's quiet and you can
run your lines with me."

He opened a door and guided Nga inside. A light turned on above
her, revealing a freshly made bed, a couple of chairs, and a vanity table.
Two sliding glass doors opened onto the warm Los Angeles right. The
man sat down on the bed and patted the place beside him.

"Come sit here, honey."

Nga did as she was told.

"How old are you?"

"I'm eleven," Nga heard herself saying in Lumen's voice.

"Really? I would have said you're at least thirteen. Maybe even
fourteen now that I'm looking at you." He looked Nga up and down.
"Your mother tells me you've been reading Tennessee Williams. That's a
little too adult, don't you think?"

"Anytime someone says something is 'too adult,' they mean it's
about sex," Nga again heard herself speaking in Lumen's voice. "What's
the big deal?"

"Oh, nothing, nothing," the man said and loosened his collar. He
shifted closer to Nga. "You are quite mature for you age, aren't you?"

Nga felt herself holding back from saying something. Instead, she
sat in the awkward silence that filled the room. Nga sighed.

"The part I have for you would require some swimming and
wearing a bathing suit. Are you a good swimmer?"

"Yes," Nga said. "We have a pool. I had lessons when I was a kid."

The man laughed. "Very good. And you don't mind wearing a
bathing suit."

"What kind of bathing suit?" Nga asked and turned to face the man. He had a long nose and pockmarked cheeks. He looked really old, maybe fifty. He seemed very sweaty, but the house was cool, air-conditioned. And nervous too. He seemed nervous. Like he was in a hurry.

"At first I would have said you'll wear a one-piece, but because you're so mature, now it's going to be a bikini."

Nga watched the man talking but said nothing.

"So, you wouldn't mind showing me your legs? I'm sure they're really very lovely, like your mother's. I can do a lighting test to see how well they'll show up on the big screen. To see if you have what it takes."

Nga stared at the man and sat more rigidly.

"It's just to see how well they'll photograph. Do you mind taking your pants off and showing me your lovely legs? It's okay. You mother knows all about this."

Nga continued to stare at the man.

"Well, if you don't want the part," he said and suddenly stood up.

"No, wait," Nga said, thawing out a little bit. "Here, I'll roll up my pant legs. Then you can see them."

"I really need to see your whole leg, not just your shins and calves," the man said as he brought a light meter out of his pocket and stood expectantly over Nga, taking readings and looking down at her.

"What's this thing right here on my pants?" Nga asked obliquely.

"What?"

"Right here on my pants," Nga indicated a spot. "What is it? Can you see it?"

"I can't from up here."

"Could you look at it?" Nga said and spread her legs open on the edge of the bed and pointed again to the spot on her pants.

The man gave Nga a weird grin and got down on his hands and knees. He shuffled over, crawling and smiling, and placed his head right between Nga's legs. He looked up at her with hungry eyes.

Nga didn't waste any time smashing her knees violently into either side of the man's head, slamming her boney kneecaps right into his temples. She did it again. And again. The man howled in pain and rolled backward onto the carpeted floor, cradling his head in his hands.

"That's what you get, you pervert!" Nga screamed at him. "I'm telling my mother right now!"

"No! Please, wait! Don't tell your mom! Don't tell *anyone!*" the man pleaded and grabbed at Nga and missed, his eyes wide, hysterical. He reached for her again, caught hold of her right arm, and pulled. But Nga felt a tug in the opposite direction. She was rising up, like a bubble from the depths of the ocean. She felt the man let go. Up and up she was traveling, slowly at first, and then quickly. She opened her eyes and was back on the ship, holding Lumen's outstretched hand.

"Woah, mate!" Nga said and leaned sideways, as if she were about to fall off the chair.

Lumen took both of Nga's hands and steadied her. "Give yourself a minute. You'll probably feel a little light-headed for a while. It's hard to go into someone's memory and come right back out."

Nga started laughing. "That creep didn't see what was coming!"

Lumen smiled and shook her head. Her shiny black hair scintillated in the ship's organic light. "My mom already taught me how to defend myself in that kind of situation. So I was totally ready for him. Even at eleven, I packed a mean right hook."

"I bet," Nga said and searched Lumen's face. "You really are *something.*"

"Thanks, but I bet you'd have done the same thing."

"I was scared to death of grown-ups," Nga said and then reached her right hand up toward Lumen's face. Lumen pulled back and watched the blue hand slowly approach and pick something off her cheek She stared blankly at Nga.

"Eyelash," Nga explained.

"Oh," Lumen said, a tiny bit flustered by the second boundary violation. "Thanks."

Nga continued, "Grown-ups were always sticking me with needles or giving me some new kind of test."

"I know what you mean. We had this woman, Dr. Albion, at Paragon...."

"What?" Nga asked, stunned. "Dr. Elizabeth Albion?"

"You too?" Lumen asked.

"White hair in a bun, always carrying a tablet or a clipboard or something with her?"

"Loves zapping people who misbehave?" Lumen asked quickly.

"That's her, all right," Nga said. "So weird!"

"How was she in Australia and Los Angeles?"

"Could be two of her?" Nga asked and made a face.

"Oh God, I hope not! One is bad enough. But you never know with Paragon. They have all kinds of tricks up their sleeves."

"She did talk about doing research on cloning...," Nga said.

"I know! She has clones of all of us back at Paragon. She tried to take our powers away and put them into those clones!"

"Weird, she didn't try that with Tyler and me, but it doesn't' surprise me one bit. She's a nasty piece of work, she is."

"Who else did you have the pleasure of meeting who worked for Paragon?" Lumen asked sarcastically.

"Top on my list would be Mammon, Leviathan, and Belphagor."

"Who?" Lumen asked.

"Oh, just your average garden-variety demons," Nga said with a grin. "Did you meet them too?"

"Oh wow! Three of them? No, but we fought Asmodeus. He's a demon too. Must be his brothers. Paragon said there were four of them."

"They're real charmers. Let me tell you. Belphagor promised to pull my heart out of my chest and eat it in front of me." Nga mimed the action.

"That's awful!" Lumen said sincerely.

"He's, like, this huge spider-demon thing with all these legs wiggling around and a head and human torso on top. But of course, he couldn't eat my heart until Paragon was done with me."

"That's some serious drama. Yeah, Asmodeus wanted to sacrifice me, I guess to the devil. He's another real asshole, just like Albion. They seemed like they were really close."

"Like lovers?"

"Maybe. It was gross watching them together," Lumen said, already a little queasy thinking about it.

"I think Albion was that way with Belphagor too. She was always flirting with him."

Nga and Lumen looked at each other with disgust on their faces. They both started laughing. James and Falling Star walked into the dining hall. They waved to Lumen to come over and join them. Kun waddled in behind them on his spindly legs. Troy and Philip came in arguing about something with the rest of the Heroes right on their heels. Their voices echoed through the dining hall.

"I guess we better go and eat?" Nga said and grinned a little bit as she stood up from the chair.

"Yeah," Lumen said and glanced up at Nga. "Let's continue this conversation later. Okay?"

"You can count on it," Nga said. "And thanks for the *suggestion*."

"No problem," Lumen said. "I can tell we're going to be great friends."

"Just friends?" Nga asked, letting the question hang in the air as she walked away and sat down with Tyler and Troy.

Lumen could feel herself blushing red as a setting sun.

6.

"THE SYZYGY will occur in thirty minutes," Kun said to the gathered Heroes. They were eating their evening meal in the ship's dining hall. Dinner consisted of Miltonian cave algae flan, soybeans with hedgehog mushrooms, and a salad of strawberries and dandelion greens. "We have much work to do, hard work. But together, we can move mountains, even *hidden* ones."

The Heroes gave out a great cheer and applauded Kun and then themselves. James was sitting on Kun's left with Falling Star and Tenzing next to him. Lumen sat across the table with Alexander, Keira, and Cedric. The other Heroes were arranged around the rest of the large dining table, eating and chattering. Even though they all had spent the last few days together, learning the plan to free the captives at the Paragon Institute, Fort Bragg, and the other US research bases around the globe, the two groups of Star Children hadn't really mingled that much. They knew each other's names, but they hadn't gotten to know each other yet. They stayed separated into two groups: the Americans and everyone else. Philip was the only one who had tried to engage with Keira, but he was rebuffed when his amorous intentions toward her became more obvious, by Cedric himself.

"Kun said during the syzygy, we take our places in the Circle of Twelve and our combined power would fuel that pendant," Keira said.

"The Eye of the Keeper," Lumen added.

"It seems simple enough," James said as he leaned close Falling Star so he would hear him over all the other talking. "I'm excited to see how it all works."

"It sounds like Kun will be very powerful," Falling Star said between bites of his dandelion greens. "I'd hate to be Paragon right now. They're going to be sorry."

"I know, right?"

"I think there's something fishy about the whole plan," Tenzing said from where he curled on Falling Star's lap.

"What? Why do you say that?" James asked.

"It's too easy," Tenzing replied casually. "Don't you think?"

"What's easy about it?" Falling Star asked. "It took Kun quite a while to get all of us Heroes together. And we all had to go to the Hidden Mountain and fight that illusion. That's really dangerous too. I'm still kind of mad about that."

"Would you stop it?" James asked, smiling. "Kun said we were all safe, and that's still true."

"But he said it was like the bardo. That's heavy."

"You know, I really did always know you were a Hero," James said proudly to Falling Star, changing the subject. "I'm sorry that you're not a Hero, Tenzing, but we still like you."

"Maybe you're just mad because you don't get to take part in this," Falling Star said to Tenzing.

Tenzing shook his striped head. "That's not it. You're so trusting. *Too* trusting. This is just like when I first found Keira. She didn't listen to her intuition at all."

"Well, I'm not worried," James added quickly. "Kun is my biological father. Why wouldn't I trust him?"

"Some father," Tenzing replied and crossed his front paws. "He never once tried to help us."

"That's not true," James said. "He helped Lumen, Paul, and me escape from Paragon by sending their cypher-lock codes hidden in Montgomery Langton poems. He told us to wait and that he'd contact us. He also told us how to find Keira up in Oakland. He did all those things."

"You sound a little paranoid," Falling Star said to Tenzing.

"I am not *paranoid*," Tenzing returned. "I am being cautious. It wouldn't hurt if all of you were a little more cautious, too, in my opinion."

"We'll let you be the cautious one," James said with a grin. "But right now, we need to get ready to fight Paragon."

Tenzing let out a long sigh, stood up, and leapt from Falling Star's lap. He trotted away from the dining hall, and off to the crew's quarters at the end of the labyrinth of ceramic hallways. He was looking for a com center or a view screen. Tenzing wanted to double-check if what Kun had said about the Circle and the Twelve Heroes was true.

It just sounds a little fishy to me, Tenzing told himself as he skittered down the hallway. *I don't know why, but I bet there must be something, some record in the ship's logs that will confirm or deny it.*

Near the end of the hall, he found what he was looking for, a vacant view screen in an empty room. He jumped up onto the ceramic ledge that ran around the chamber and walked quickly to locate the glass thought-pad. The view screen cast an eerie glow around the room as Tenzing approached. He placed his front paws on the thought-pad and asked his query with his mind: The Circle of Twelve.

The response came back as a disembodied voice.

"The Circle of Twelve is a magic space used by practitioners of Zetan ritual magic. It is generally believed that the Circle contains sacred energy which can be manipulated by the talisman, the Eye of the Keeper. The Circle itself is a sacred space, which can also provide a form of magical protection. When the Twelve Heroes are seated in the Circle during the alignment of certain planets, a powerful superbeing is created, the *Frábær Vera*."

The voice paused. *"Do you want me to tell you more?"*

"No, thank you. I've heard enough," Tenzing replied.

"The Sumerians called the practice of using magic circles Zisurru." the voice continued.

"That's enough," Tenzing said quickly. "Thank you."

"Are you sure you don't want to hear more? I've got loads and loads of information about all sorts of subjects."

"No, really, thank you," Tenzing replied, getting a little bit flustered.

"It's just that I'm so lonely," the voice continued. "No one comes to this part of the ship very much anymore."

"I'm sorry to hear that," Tenzing said. "I'll let them know to come down and talk to you more often."

"Would you do that for me? Really" The view screen turned a warm pink color, as if blushing.

"Sure, it's no problem," Tenzing said. "But I should be leaving."

"Okay, See you later, *friend*."

Ugh, that's all we need, clingy AI. Well, all that stuff about the Circle checks out. Kun wasn't making it up. Maybe I am being a little paranoid. But they're just a bunch of teenagers, and I'm an old man, Tenzing reassured himself. *It's my job to second-guess them.*

He sighed again, hopped down from the ledge, and walked quickly back out into the hallway, the view screen blinking goodbye behind him.

JAMES WATCHED Tenzing leaving the dinner table, then looked up at Falling Star. He made a disbelieving face, and James quietly giggled.

"Tenzing is in a weird mood."

"What are you two talking about?" Kun asked as he walked up and leaned his bulbous head into the conversation. He stared at them with unblinking eyes.

"Nothing," James said.

"I hope you aren't worried about this action we're taking against the US government and Paragon."

"I'm not," James said and turned to face Kun.

"How about you, Falling Star?"

The yeti prince shook his head and smiled.

"Good. You have nothing to worry about. Once all the Heroes are in their places in the circle, I will channel your combined powers through the Eye of the Keeper. We will be unstoppable." Kun lifted the medallion and its dark crystal up in front of him. It glimmered in the pale light from the spaceship's walls. "Paragon have no idea what's coming for them."

"I'm just excited to get started," James said. "I want to free the prisoners Paragon is keeping against their will and experimenting on."

"We'll take care of all of them," Kun said and patted James lightly on the shoulder. "I'll see you two in the Circle."

"We'll be there."

As Kun turned to leave, James asked, "Paul is the last Hero, right? Did he make it back from the Hidden Mountain?"

"Paul will be there at the Circle, too," Kun said, smiled, and walked away.

"Lumen is not going to like that," James said.

"Maybe she won't notice?" Falling Star asked.

"Won't notice?" James replied. "It would be hard not to notice Paul."

"Well, we don't have to tell her right away."

"I guess not, but she's not going to be happy," James said, shaking his head.

AFTER DINNER, Lumen walked into the room she shared with Keira. Red thoughtforms scattered and went down the hallway behind her. Keira was already dressed in her ceremonial clothes for the appearance of the Circle of Twelve. She sat on her latticework bed and pulled on a pair of silver boots. Keira glanced up for a moment as Lumen entered.

"Are we still talking?" Keira asked.

"Why wouldn't we be?"

"You seemed really mad earlier," Keira said as she tugged her left boot into place.

"Not mad," Lumen began. "I think disappointed is a better word."

"It happens," Keira said frankly. "Cedric and I really like each other."

"I could see that."

"It doesn't mean that I feel any less for you. You're still my BFF."

Lumen stared at Keira for a moment. "Don't best friends tell each other everything?"

"I am telling you," Keira said with a little fluster. "Cedric and I would like to try to be a couple."

"Why do I feel like you guys are dumping me?"

"We're not. I swear. Neither of us expected this."

Lumen looked over at Keira on the bed.

"Really, the last person I wanted to hurt would be you, Lumen."

"I know. I'm just being stupid. I always knew this could happen," Lumen said with a deep sigh. "But I didn't know it would hurt like this. I thought we were being careful to keep it casual."

"And now it seems so serious, *right*?"

"Yeah. I thought we were going to stay open and unattached." Lumen pulled her ceremonial bodysuit out of the metallic closet and put it on quickly. Purple lights blinked along the walls as energy pulsed through the ship's body.

"I guess the human heart only works one way," Keira replied.

"One love at a time?"

"Yeah."

Lumen was silent for a moment, thinking. "One of the other Heroes was really flirty with me earlier."

"Really?" Keira said and perked up. "Who was it? Not Philip?"

Lumen shook her head and then grimaced. "It was that girl from New Zealand, Nga."

"Wow, she seems really cool."

"She's…." Lumen started to say something but couldn't find the right word. "Complicated."

"Who isn't? Look at Cedric," Keira said. "He's got issues with his parents, just like me."

"But we're okay," Lumen assured Keira. "I'm cool with you and Cedric being together."

"I'm so glad," Keira said, getting a little teary-eyed. "Losing you would be too much for me to bear."

James walked into the ceramic room as Lumen and Keira were hugging. "Didn't mean to interrupt."

"You didn't," Keira said, wiping away a happy tear as she let go of Lumen.

"We're all going to the aft deck to wait for the Circle of Twelve."

Lumen adjusted both her sleeves, pulling them down to her wrists. "Why can't they make these things fit better?"

"Didn't Kun tell you? That's part of the ritual," James said, grinning. "You have to dance around, throwing your arms into the air, to wiggle into your ceremonial suit."

"Yours fits you just fine," Keira said.

James looked handsome in his metallic suit. It was decorated with hand-painted Zetan hieroglyphs, the same as the ones the girls wore. There were no pockets or zippers. The fabric simply wrapped around his body like paint poured onto a sculpture; it covered him with a glittering layer of silver.

"That's because I'm not curvy like you are."

"Yeah," Lumen added. "It's like dressing a bookmark with James."

"I'm not that skinny!"

"But you are, Blanche," Lumen said, doing her best crazy Bette Davis impression. "You are."

The three of them laughed, remembering the line from that campy film *Whatever Happened to Baby Jane?* Then they were quiet for a moment. That film, and their old lives in the real world back on Earth, away from Paragon, away from all of this, seemed so far off now. Here they were in Kun's spaceship, orbiting the planet Venus, waiting to attack the US government with an unearthly force and free all the prisoners and Star Children from the clutches of Dr. Albion and General Hesslop. Without saying anything, the three of them joined hands. A feeling of home, of security and love passed between them. They knew that no matter what, they would always have each other. They looked across the circle of their arms and bodies and into each other's eyes.

Falling Star stepped into the room and then stopped in his tracks. "Forgive me for intruding like this."

Lumen, Keira, and James laughed and let go of each other's hands. "Today is the day for interruptions," Lumen said. "Right, James?"

"It's just that Kun told me to get you three because the Circle has just materialized and he needs us all there," Falling Star said with excitement in his deep voice.

"Already?" James said. "We're ahead of schedule."

"We're ready," Lumen said.

A new cloud of Zetan thoughtforms zigzagged down the hallway behind Falling Star. It looked like a flock of fuchsia butterflies flitting about.

"Let's go," James said and walked over and grabbed Falling Star's large hand. "After you."

Falling Star smiled and headed toward the aft deck.

"IT LOOKS like they ripped out someone's patio and dropped it down over there," James said as the Heroes began to gather around the Circle of Twelve. Inside the ship's large ceramic aft chamber, a huge carved stone disk, about fifty feet in diameter, had been positioned on the floor. It seemed oddly out of place against all the alien tech that surrounded it on the walls and blinking instrument panels. Velvet moss grew across the surface of the stone disk, and some kind of vine crept over it in vein-like patterns.

Kun stood at a metallic panel along the back wall. Above his head, two large 3D maps of the United States and one of the entire globe were projected into the room. Red points blinked on the maps, Kun's targets: US Army bases and their international laboratories. Another projection showed the planets in the solar system lining up in syzygy. It was time. He waved all the Heroes over to him.

"It's time!" Kun began, excitement in his voice.

"What are we looking for?" James asked.

"Watch the circle!" Kun touched his pendant, and the stone disk started to glow with a faint purple light and emit a low humming sound. The purple light increased in brightness and the sound became louder until shapes of chairs, twelve of them, materialized across the glowing circle. The outlines had high backs and looked more like thrones than chairs. Slowly each one came into focus and became a physical object right in front of them.

"That is the coolest thing I've ever seen," Paul said as he strolled up behind Lumen, Keira, Falling Star, Cedric, and James.

"Who let you out?" Lumen asked.

"Duh, I'm still a Hero, in case you haven't noticed," Paul replied with a bit of a sneer, which he quickly dropped when James shot him a look. "I'm the twelfth. You need me to unlock the Circle's power. Didn't Kun tell you?"

"Well, you better be on your best behavior," Lumen said quickly. "I don't want you messing everything up."

"Would you relax?" Paul said. "Didn't James tell you about my implant?"

"Yeah, that's a little convenient," Keira said.

"You don't believe me?"

"It's not about *believe*. It's about *trust*," Lumen said. "I don't trust you."

"That's something I can work on," Paul said. "I'll get you to trust me again. I certainly don't want to go back to the Hidden Mountain again. That place made me lose my appetite forever."

"Was it really bad?" James asked.

"Yeah, I think I'm going to be a vegetarian from now on."

"Yeah, you do that," Lumen replied and turned away.

Kun stood across the Circle and waved his skinny arms. "It's time, Heroes. Please line up single file next to me. This is the entrance to the Circle. It's very important you approach in this way, individually, or we will spoil the incantation. Remember, once you enter, look for your energy crystal. You will know it by its color. You'll feel it. It will appear over your seat."

TENZING WALKED quickly back through the ceramic hallways that led to the crew's quarters. Floating thoughtforms glittered on the ceiling, landing here and there, their hidden senders letting the ship know what to do. Tenzing was too preoccupied to pay too much attention to them. Even though he knew what Kun had said was the truth, he still had a bad feeling he just couldn't shake.

Out of the corner of his yellow cat's eye, Tenzing saw something large with black-and-white markings duck into the crew's quarters. The lighting was dim in the hallway, with only the occasional glow of electric current through the walls and the faint light from the thoughtforms, but Tenzing knew what he saw. It looked like a demon. And not just any demon, but Mara, or as he now called himself, Asmodeus. He shook his head and looked again. His eyes cut right through the gloom like a pair of night-vision googles.

How could he have found us here? No one knows what happened to the crew of Project Darkfeather. Maybe it was a trick of the light? I better check it out just in case.

Tenzing slunk down the hallway, flattening himself against the wall as he approached the round doorway. He carefully stuck his head into the room.

Nothing. Latticework beds, a few moon chairs. Nothing out of the ordinary.

Then Tenzing had the sudden sensation of flying, and the realization that someone had just grabbed him by the collar and yanked him upward.

"Ahh, Little Monk," Asmodeus said as he dangled the cat before him. "We meet again. But this time, I'm ready for you."

"Put me down this instant!" Tenzing shrieked, struggling. "You have no right to be here!"

"Oh yes, I do. I have every right."

"I'm going to send you back to Hell for good this time!"

"You can try, Little Monk, but you'll find I have the upper hand."

Something glittering on Tenzing's collar attracted Asmodeus's eye. "What's this?" he said and lifted the cat closer to his face.

Tenzing arched his back and hissed as loudly as he could manage. He glared at the demon's scorched face.

"This green stone hanging from your collar. What is it?" the demon asked. "This is no ordinary stone. I can sense something odd about it. It feels like Bodhisattva magic. Who gave it to you?"

Tenzing crossed his front paws over his chest and turned his head away.

"You're not going to tell me? Fine. I'll analyze it myself." With that, Asmodeus plucked the stone off Tenzing's collar. It began to glow bright emerald between his fingers.

"Give that back!" Tenzing screeched at the demon and thrashed his paws through the air, claws out, trying to grab back the stone. "It's of no use to you. Give it back to me!"

"No," Asmodeus replied calmly as he slipped the green stone into a small pouch he wore at his hip. "Its magic must be very powerful or you wouldn't want it so badly."

"James! Lumen! Keira!" Tenzing threw back his head and called out in his alley cat voice, but no one was near enough to hear. "Someone help me!"

"Enough of that!" Asmodeus said, and then without hesitating, stuffed Tenzing into a plexiglass cage that was waiting beside him on the floor.

The cat squirmed and fought but was eventually subdued and locked into the cage. Tenzing hissed and howled again at the top of his lungs.

"It's no use. This cage is completely sound- and thought-proof. Remote viewing is not possible. Lumen can't find you. Oh yes, you can hear me, too, but no one can hear you." Asmodeus lifted the cage up so he was eye to eye with Tenzing. "You can chant any sutra you want, but you're not sending me back anywhere." The demon grinned, exposing his daggerlike chipped teeth.

The cat frantically threw himself at the cage door, banging into it again and again.

"You're going to give yourself a concussion, Little Monk. Can't you see you're caught?" The demon lowered the cage and began walking down the hallway, heading deep into the heart of Kun's ship. "Not to worry," Asmodeus announced as the cage bounced against his thigh. "You'll be out of there in no time. There's someone I want you to meet. He's Serpian. He's really going to love eating you," the demon said and then paused to correct himself. "I mean, he'll love *meeting* you."

Tenzing's mind raced. What could he do? Asmodeus had the secret stone that EBE had given him. This was it, the bad feeling he had! He really was at the mercy of the demon. Tenzing had to get away to warn James and the other Heroes. But how?

JAMES STOOD at the head of the line before the glowing circle and its twelve chairs. He had the oddest feeling of déjà vu, as if he'd done this before, in some other time, some other life.

But that's impossible, isn't it? James thought.

He turned to look at the Heroes assembled behind him. Lumen, Keira, and Alexander smiled at him. Falling Star also grinned warmly back at James. Paul and Cedric were talking with Philip and didn't notice James watching them. Nga and Tyler both had looks of excitement on their faces. Troy and Stephen made up the end of the line, and both seemed a little more nervous than the others. But the buzz of a new adventure was in the air all around them.

"Didn't Tenzing want to be here to see this?" Lumen asked.

"Yeah, he only left a little while ago," James said.

"Where is he anyway?" Keira asked. "I can't feel him."

"Let me see," Lumen said and closed her eyes to concentrate. She held her fingers to her temples, focusing her energy. "I'm not seeing him anywhere on the ship."

"Touch my arm and boost your power," Keira suggested.

"Okay," Lumen replied and did as Keira suggested.

"What do you mean you can't see him?" James asked. "He's got to be on the ship."

Kun strolled quickly up to James and Lumen. "It's time, James. You need to enter the Circle."

"But we can't find Tenzing," Keira said, worry shaking in her voice.

"Yeah, he wanted to be here to see this," James said.

"Before you ask, we can't wait for him. I'm sorry he's going to miss it," Kun said with a note of hurrying in his voice. "But he can watch the recordings we're making. We have to do this before the syzygy is over."

"But why can't I find him?" Lumen asked as she opened her eyes and looked directly into Kun's huge black ones, trying to read him.

"There are places on the ship that are dead zones for remote viewing. He's probably inside one of them," Kun responded.

Lumen couldn't get a fix on Kun's thoughts as hard as she tried. They were sliding about, unreadable. She figured he was anxious and that caused his mental haze. They were all anxious. Nothing to worry about.

"Maybe he's sleeping," James suggested hopefully.

"It just feels weird that I can't locate him, even with Keira's power boosting mine."

"I'm afraid we'll have to figure this out later," Kun said, his frustration clear on his face. "Please, we have to do this now."

"Okay," James said. "He's right. We'll have to figure this out later."

"James, please take your place," Kun again insisted. "Enter the Circle. I'll summon the Circle Keeper."

Kun rubbed the strange amulet that hung around his neck, and it hummed loudly with an eerie sound, like the combination of a cicada's buzz and the shrill call of a dolphin. The Heroes all held their ears at the same time, trying to block out the maddening noise. Then, as quickly as it had started, the sound stopped. Silence radiated from the amulet, and then it glowed. A golden beam of light shone from its jewel onto the stone circle. A large archway sprang up in front of them. It breathed and moved with energy. Two eyes blinked open on its topmost stones and glared down at the line of Heroes.

"Who dares to call on me?" the Keeper bellowed.

"It is I, Kun, brother of EBE, Keisari of Hjarta."

"Yes, Kun, brother of EBE, what do you wish of the Circle of Twelve?"

"To vanquish the enemies of Hjarta and free the prisoners of Paragon."

"Do you have the Twelve Heroes assembled? Are they tried and true and pure of heart?" the Keeper asked, his eyes looking over the assembled teenagers.

"Yes. They are waiting to take their places."

"Let it be so," the Circle Keeper said and closed his eyes. The energy archway trembled and then became solid stone, frozen in time.

James looked over at Kun, who smiled at him faintly. He swallowed hard, trying to push down his fear. James took two steps forward and then looked back and at the rest of the Heroes waiting in line for their turn. They were all now as nervous as he was.

As James approached the archway, he felt the oddest sensation, but one he'd felt before. It was the same feeling as the first time he approached Y'Luc; the Circle of Twelve recognized him. It welcomed him. He knew instinctively, as the bright white crystal began to glow over the fifth chair on the right, that this was his place. He passed under the stone archway, and immediately all he wanted to do was join his energy to the Circle. It was an overwhelming sensation. It felt wonderful. James became indivisible from the stone chairs, the slabs of moss-covered granite beneath his feet, and the mortar that held all of it together. He quickly walked to his chair and sat.

"One to the first power," the Keeper's voice said in James's head.

He adjusted his hands on the armrests and squeezed the carved stonework, as if making himself more a part of it.

Lumen entered the circle, and James could feel her all at once, and she him. They stared at each other, suddenly one body. The violet crystal began to glow over the sixth chair on the right. Lumen joined James in the circle.

"Two to the second power," the Keeper again sounded in their combined consciousnesses.

Keira stepped into the circle and was swept up in the belonging. Three bodies became one, three minds became one, three hearts became one. The emerald stone glowed over the fourth chair to the left. Keira sat immediately and melded with the Circle's energy.

"Three to the third power," the Keeper's voice again announced.

Philip slunk into the Circle and joined the fused energies, the blended awarenesses. He sat beneath the amber stone that glowed over the fifth chair on the left, next to Keira, and across from Lumen and James.

"Four to the fourth power."

The stones in the Circle glowed even brighter.

The rest of the Heroes on their own turns joined into the circle of stone chairs. Nga joined last and sat in the chair beneath the glowing opal, sixth chair on the right.

"Twelve to the twelfth power. The Circle is complete. Touch the Eye of the Keeper to command its energies."

The Twelve Heroes watched each other through each other's eyes. Their sentience shifted from one body to another, then to two bodies, three bodies, splitting and dividing itself between them, four bodies, seven bodies, eleven bodies, lingering, thinking, remembering, twelve bodies. The sensation swirled through them and was all-encompassing. They had melded with each other, the Circle, and the universe. They were connected to every atom in every direction.

And then they sensed it, all at the same time: They were frozen in their seats.

They couldn't move.

Trapped!

Not a single muscle, not even their tongues to speak.

And then something shifted close by, something on the ship, and a negative energy emerged. They could all sense it. As they looked up to find

Kun still standing a few feet away from the Circle, Asmodeus walked out and stood next to him. His naked body seemed different, blacker and more charred than before, with only a few streaks of white zigzagging across his flesh. He said something to Kun that they couldn't hear.

Kun and the demon both laughed.

From behind a folding screen in the corner of the chamber, Dr. Elizabeth Albion appeared. She walked carefully over and took her place next to Kun and Asmodeus. She smiled at the Heroes, her ex-test subjects, imprisoned within the Circle.

A ripple of fear spread out over the Heroes. Keira looked across at Lumen, who tried to turn to look at James.

It's her! James thought to everyone.

What are those two doing here? Keira thought back.

Lumen glared at the demon and the doctor. *Cedric—can you still use your powers?*

Yes—a little.

Keira, send some amplification to Cedric. I want you to read the Circle. I need to know more about it so we can figure out how to defeat it.

Keira focused what little energy she still had, that wasn't being drawn into the Circle, on Cedric. He found he could still move the fingers on his left hand. He felt down onto the armrest of the stone chair. Something brushed his finger. It felt like beef jerky, some kind of dried-up meat. As he began to read the substance, his thoughts traveled across the Circle.

"I can see Albion," he started to say as the memory fed itself into the consciousness of the group and began to play out.

The image clarified. It was Fort Bragg, CA, in a bunker deep beneath the ground, a few years ago. Dr. Albion held her iPad to her chest as she watched her most recent clutch of clones take their places in the stone Circle. The syzygy was in full effect over the base. It was satisfying to know that these impostors were biologically identical to the Star Children she'd been chasing around the globe for so many years now. The whole reason the Star Children were created in the first place was for this purpose—to harness the energy of the Circle of Twelve.

True, she'd been able to weaponize many of their test subjects, use them against the enemies of the United States. But their real function was here, to unlock the Circle. Dr. Albion delighted in a James Kerr that looked and acted like the real James Kerr but didn't disobey her every command; a Keira Darkfeather identical to the real Keira but much more subservient. All Twelve Heroes had been reproduced in clone form, powers and all, from various genetic samples Paragon had collected.

Dr. Albion had seen to that.

She glanced down at her tablet. The planets were now aligned above the base. Having bases all around the globe made it easier to find a place where the syzygy would be occurring. This year it happened over the West Coast of the United States. This was the time to summon the Circle Keeper. All of her research led up to this. And with only their clones, she was going to activate the power of the Circle and use it for her benefit.

As the clone Troy, the last Star Child to enter into the circle, took his place in the last stone chair, a strange humming sound began from within the stones.

"Are you recording this?" Dr. Albion shouted to a hidden camera operator. "This is it! What we've been waiting for. General Hesslop, your money has been well spent."

The stone circle began to glow bright white, its intensity rising with the sound of the humming. The Lumen clone shifted and made the first cry of pain. She gasped and shook her dark hair down into her face, her shoulders thrust back against the glowing chair. She threw back her head, mouth falling open, and let out a deafening scream.

"Something's happening!" Dr. Albion shouted over the noise.

The light seemed to envelop the clone's form, flashing and swirling red and purple over her legs and chest, then down her arms to her pointed fingertips. The humming stopped as the glowing intensified, now too bright to look at. The Lumen clone froze completely, staring straight ahead. Her synthetic sternum cracked open, yellowish blood flooding out, and the clone looked over at Dr. Albion with confusion on its face, and then it exploded. Artificial flesh sprayed across the Circle and the other clones, as they, too, one by one, screamed and exploded.

"No! This can't be happening! All my work! All those years of research! My precious clones!"

As the last Star Child burst, its rubberized insides flying out over the Circle, Dr. Albion threw her tablet to the ground and stomped on it with her Jimmy Choo high heels.

The memory began to spool itself back inside of Cedric's mind. The Star Children looked around at the dried bits of flesh hanging from the sides of the thrones.

I thought it was moss or something, James thought to everyone.

You mean, all that stuff is dead clone goop? Nga asked.

It sure looks like it, Lumen answered. *I had no idea that Albion loved her clones so much.*

I'm glad we got rid of ours back at that theater in Oakland, Paul thought.

Not all of ours, Keira thought back. *Lumen's got away.*

They couldn't hold the energy of the Circle, Tyler said suddenly in his mind and then laughed. *Dr. Albion has only had failures.*

I guess that shows humans will always be better than clones, James replied to the group.

Hey, look, Lumen said. *Kun is watching us. He knows we're talking to each other.*

As Lumen thought the final words of the sentence, Kun came ambling over, his head wobbling from side to side. "Yes, my children, I do owe you an explanation, don't I? I know you're talking telepathically. But I didn't lie to you. We *will* liberate all the prisoners at Paragon as I promised," Kun said as an evil smile now ran across his lopsided face. "As you have no doubt guessed, I will siphon off your combined energies, draining you down to your last living drop. For some of you, this will be the last day of your usefulness to Paragon. This will be your last day to be *alive*."

Kun watched the expressions on the Star Children trapped in the Circle. "You can only imagine how powerful I will be. Twelve to the twelfth power. I'll focus that energy through the amulet. I will turn the US government's prisoners, all those people in every Sculpture Garden, in every secret base, into my indestructible foot soldiers. I will use them to subdue every army, conquer every government, until, finally, *I will rule this planet.*"

Dr. Albion laughed loudly and joined Kun, patting him on the shoulder.

"The government had no idea that one day you'd turn their Sculpture Gardens against them. This is a red-letter day, my friend!" Dr. Albion said gleefully. "I can't believe the Star Children fell for this so easily. They've been nothing but trouble to me. Especially that one." Dr. Albion pointed at James. "I will certainly delight in his death."

Asmodeus walked up and stood looking at Keira and Lumen. "I want the reward you promised me."

"Of course, Asmodeus," Dr. Albion said smoothly. "Those two girls are yours when we finish here. In fact, why don't we throw in Nga? I'm sure she'll make a wonderful blood sacrifice."

"It will take a few hours, maybe a whole day, before we have total control of the Earth. Really, it will only be a matter of how long the Heroes can stay alive in the Circle as we drain away their life-energies."

This can't be happening! James thought.

Well, it is! Lumen thought back.

What are we going to do? Troy asked the circle of Star Children.

We've got to get out of the Circle and stop them, James thought back.

And then James knew it, somehow, deep inside of himself. This was the end. Kun had total control over them and unlimited access to their abilities. James looked down at his arms, melded to his throne, and then glanced up at Falling Star just in time to see the first tear fall from his eye.

But where is Tenzing? He's still on the ship somewhere. Maybe he can help us? James thought quickly.

That lazy cat is probably still asleep somewhere, Paul said.

Like you know anything about him, Lumen said. *You should stay out of this.*

Um, hello, Ms. Kim! Can't you see I'm trapped here too? You didn't see Dr. Albion trying to save me, did you? They're going to destroy me too.

That's a relief, anyway, Lumen thought.

We're in this together, Paul shot back.

That's what I was afraid of, Lumen said.

7.

TENZING LOOKED around the strange room he was held captive in. Asmodeus had pulled him out of the cage and tossed into the room and then locked the door. Tenzing started howling, trying to get someone's attention, anyone's.

Lumen! Where are you? Pick up my thoughts! Lumen, please answer me! Asmodeus is here! You are all in grave danger! Tenzing's panic ran feverishly around his brain. *Keira! Can you feel my fear? Can you feel our connection?*

He paced the room. No way out except the door. A dim light glowed from an unseen source above him.

It must be motion-activated, Tenzing thought.

The room was empty, no bed or chairs. There was nothing except for a dark puddle of something in the far corner. Tenzing imagined that a previous prisoner must have relieved themselves over there. He turned and walked over to the door. It was closed and locked and wouldn't budge. He stretched up on his hind legs and looked at the smooth surface.

No hinges or latches to unlock. Just a small space beneath the door, and I'm definitely not skinny enough get out that way.

Tenzing heard a faint gurgling sound behind him. He turned to see the dark patch on the floor begin to undulate and trickle. It rippled and flowed toward him like molten tar.

What is that? I don't like the looks of it. Get me out of here!

Tenzing rushed to the farthest corner of the room to get away from the advancing black goo. He turned and arched his back, hissing loudly. The black substance came at him more quickly, long black streaks rushing forward from the wiggling mass like the lengths of tentacles trying to grab him. Tenzing jumped over the quivering blob, its black feelers reaching up and missing him as he leapt.

He landed in the center of the room and quickly turned to see his attacker. The roiling slime bubbled and frothed, rushing forward. It contracted into a thin black rivulet and ran at Tenzing. He dodged the advancing stream to the right, only to find the creature stretching up the length of its body like a long black wall, which towered above him and then came down, falling over his body in a sticky sheet. Everything went black.

The burning sting of acid began immediately as Tenzing felt the digestive enzymes flooding out of the black ooze onto his furry body. He writhed in agony as his flesh separated from his bones. The black ooze quivered wildly. His one last conscious thought rose and fell into a wave of pain, and then confusion swallowed him.

The burning blackness inside the blob turned into deadly, cold silence.

"I'VE SUMMONED my brothers," Asmodeus said to Kun. "They should be here any second."

"Good, we're going to need all the demonic help we can get," Kun replied as he turned his attention from the glowing map of the world. "And now, to the Circle." Kun indicated the ring of stone chairs and the trapped Star Children with his skinny hand. "It's time to set this plan in motion."

"So many years I've waited," Dr. Albion said in a breathy voice that was almost a hiss. "And now to have my revenge on all those who doubted me. *Those tiny fools!*"

Behind them, sulfurous smoke began to billow from beneath slatted floor panels. Electric sparks flashed and snapped in the yellow cloud. A thunderclap rang through the ship as orange lightning flashed brightly. As quickly as it arrived, the smoke vanished, revealing three large beings, Asmodeus's brothers, the other Princes of the Underworld.

James shot a disbelieving look at Lumen. *Who are they?*

Nga answered, *Those are the demons Paragon works with, Asmodeus's brothers. They're the ones who came after us down under.*

Fear pulsed around the stone circle.

Their names are Mammon, Leviathan, and Belphagor.

Mammon, the first, was nothing more than a huge floating brain the size of a sports car. He had a long, bony spinal cord hanging down from behind him and a pair of glowing red eyes on stalks that emerged from the brain's frontal lobes. The whole brain dripped with transparent slime. Leviathan, the second, stood as tall as Asmodeus, about seven feet, Falling Star's height. He was muscular, but it was hard to tell beneath his pale gray flesh that wrinkled and puckered over him as if he were wearing someone else's ill-fitting skin. Belphagor, the third demon, was bigger than his other two brothers, his face green beneath a pair of spreading insect mandibles, his muscular torso attached to a hairy spider's body.

"Your brothers' timing is impeccable," Kun said with an evil smile. "They arrived just in time to see me summon the energy from the Circle. Places, everyone. Please take your seats so no one gets hurt."

Dr. Albion, followed closely by the four demons, sauntered over to a row of what looked like enormous beanbag chairs. The doctor sat quickly in the first one, her small body swallowed up by the squishy material. She struggled to reach over and pull a safety belt across her lap and fasten it.

"Oh, Belphy, it's been too long," Dr. Albion said jovially as she sat back against the lumpy seat.

"Yes, Elizabeth. We have missed your flesh," the spidery demon replied, his legs tapping on the ceramic floor as he squatted down, positioning his hairy abdomen over the soft chair. "What pleasures we have to show you."

"Indeed!" Dr. Albion said.

"Quiet, everyone," Kun scolded as he positioned himself in front of the Circle's gateway. "I need to concentrate."

"Pardon me," Dr. Albion said sarcastically as she turned to wink at Belphagor. Mammon sat curled in a seat, his spinal cord wrapped around his frontal lobe, while Leviathan stretched himself out across his chair, his hands beneath the back of his head, his flabby skin pooling beneath his joints, elbows and knees.

Kun returned his attention to the Circle. He lifted up his amulet with both hands and aimed it at the Heroes. Kun began to recite the incantation, the amulet glowing brightly with an eerie blue-white light. "Tributo sanguinis hominum vivi et voto sacrificii hominis unius aut plurium, depeciscor cum daemone ad servitutem eius volentis. Aperto mentem meam ad tuam. Iuva me ut potestates horum liberorum duodecim tollam!"

HE'S SPEAKING *in Latin,* Lumen said, her mind instantly translating the conjuring spell for the others. *It's something about freeing his mind and summoning a demon to steal all of our powers and give them to him.*

The stone circle vibrated. A whirling sensation, like being inside an angry tornado, shook the chairs beneath the Heroes. The rushing sound of wind filled their ears. The spiritual gemstones appeared over their heads and beamed their energies into Kun's amulet.

It hurts! James shouted in his mind as his bioelectric charge drained from his body. *I can't stop it. It's like I'm bleeding out!*

Fight it! Lumen said to the group. *It's our only chance. Fight the Circle!*

I can't! Keira gasped. *It's too powerful! It's like my insides are being turned out!*

Focus! Lumen said. *If we focus our powers away from the Circle, we might be able to break free.*

My head is going to explode! Stephen shouted.

Kun looked at the pained faces of the Heroes trapped in the Circle and smiled. He could feel the amulet filling with their powers. Each moment it sucked away their life forces, combining them into a more powerful energy for Kun to command. He glanced back at his guests, strapped into their chairs, as the violent winds from the Circle howled past them at hurricane force, blowing dust and bits of moss around the ship. Mammon's eyestalks bobbed; Leviathan's folds of skin flapped wildly at his sides. Asmodeus and Belphagor held tightly to Dr. Albion, whose white lab coat waved like a flag. She looked like she would blow away, had it not been the powerful grip of the two demon brothers.

Try to withstand it! Lumen yelled with her mind. *Focus on your powers, not the pain!* As soon as the last word echoed around the circle, Lumen felt it. She was being engulfed by the stone chair. The more the amulet pulled her life force out of her, the more the stone encroached into her flesh. The cold rush of marble moved up through her legs, up her spine and into her torso, down her arms and into her hands, and finally up the back of her neck and into her brain.

Then stillness. Stillness and silence.

Lumen could see everything, but she couldn't hear, speak, or send out telepathic messages to the others. Her consciousness struggled inside the grip of stone.

No use. I'm trapped.

The others around the Circle were also now encased by mottled marble and limestone. Their bodies had become an enormous sculpture, a symbol of the wickedness of Kun and Paragon.

Kun threw his spindly arms into the air, gave a loud gasp as a huge blue flash emanated from the stone circle and penetrated the amulet. He took two steps back and caught his breath. The air calmed, and the room again filled with stony silence. Kun looked around the ship and then down at the amulet. It glowed a sickening moldy blue color. "It's done!" he screamed. "I am the master of all their powers!"

Dr. Albion wasted no time in unfastening her safety belt and rushing to Kun's side. The demons followed.

"Quickly, let's start Phase One of the takeover," Dr. Albion said breathlessly. "You two—go monitor the US military bases," she said to Mammon and Leviathan, who complied by moving in front of the large viewing screen on the wall and punching in the coordinates. Mammon used his dripping spinal cord to tap out the locations on the keyboard.

"I'll watch the Chinese military bases," Belphagor said and located a screen to sit before.

"You two stay with me," Kun said. "I need to focus my energies down to Earth. You'll need to be here if something goes wrong."

"What could go wrong? We've been planning this for years...." Dr. Albion started to say until Kun shot her a withering glance.

"I need protection while I'm in a trance and sending my energy down to the planet's surface. Who knows if those Heroes are really out of commission?"

"They don't look too perky," Asmodeus said with a toothy grin. "I wouldn't worry about them ever again. They are permanently sidelined."

"Nevertheless, I need you here protecting me while I'm in that vulnerable state."

"It's true, out here, anything could collide with us: a comet, some rogue satellite," Dr. Albion added.

"The Nibiru object," Asmodeus said, and both he and the doctor laughed heartily.

"Would you two *stop* joking around? I have to concentrate."

"Of course, you are right," Dr. Albion said finally as she winked at the demon.

"I can see everything," Leviathan said as he moved a fleshy fold covering his right eye. "The entire US military complex is going about its business. They have no idea what's coming."

"Excellent," Kun said and clapped his three-fingered hands. "Now let's get down to business." Kun took up the amulet and placed it against his forehead. "It begins!"

He squeezed his eyes shut, deep in concentration. Circles of blue energy began rolling like hoops out of the amulet and right through the walls of the ship. Dr. Albion moved up to a panel in the wall and called up the outside camera feeds. Through the cosmic darkness and the pinpricks of stars, blue energy rings were rolling away from the ship and straight at the Earth.

"Oh, this is all too perfect," she said and walked over and threw her arms around Asmodeus. "We will rule Earth together, my infernal prince."

"It's only a matter of time," Asmodeus replied and slipped his huge, charred arm around Dr. Albion's waist and drew her close to his naked form.

"Now we watch and wait," Dr. Albion said as she stretched up to kiss the demon on the lips and tasted blood and sulfur.

PRIVATE BEN Bondsol punched in the code on the touchpad and opened the door to the "Sculpture Garden." It was only his second week at Paragon, and he had not gotten used to checking on the psychic prisoners whose biometric energy ran the entire underground base. They had been isolated and sedated because their powers made them too dangerous, and Paragon had failed to control them any other way. They were one part battery and one part human bonsai. Their bodies had been hardened against the softening of time and underuse, their muscles still strong and flexible thanks to a reverse-engineered alien elixir.

The Sculpture Garden was the cruel name this open prison was given.

The overhead lights blinked on, sensing Bondsol's movements below them. Before him stretched out row after row of silent bodies: men, women, even a few children, hundreds of naked bodies packed into a space the size of an airplane hangar. They had all been weapons of the US government, remote viewing, neutralizing enemy targets, using their powers to bring down governments. Now multicolored tubes and wires ran from the ceiling down into each of their waiting bodies. Their skin tone was a sickly gray from the chemicals that kept them barely alive in a coma-like state and the years spent underground away from sunlight. Even though Bondsol knew they were in suspended animation, he still hated this assignment. His first time here, one of them coughed, purely a muscular reflex, but it scared the hell out of him. Since then, each shift here filled him with dread. A trickle of cold sweat ran down his neck and between his shoulder blades.

"Bondsol!" his walkie-talkie blared, making him jump. "Come in. What's your twenty?"

"In the Sculpture Garden, sir," Bondsol answered as he pressed the large black button on the side of the walkie-talkie. A shiver went through his entire body. "Everything is quiet down here."

"What? *Of course* it's quiet down there. What else would those stiffs be doing?"

"I don't know, sir."

"Hurry up and finish your patrol, Private. General Hesslop has need of an assistant," the voice on the walkie-talkie snapped. "Over and out."

Bondsol wiped his brow. It was clammy with cold sweat. To his left, deep in the ranks of the bodies, he heard a moan. Just a short sound. Nothing really, like a gasp. "It's just a reflex," he reminded himself. "I'll check the other side of the room and I'll be done."

As Private Bondsol walked along the rows, he had the distinct feeling he was being watched. He stopped in his tracks and searched across the tethered bodies. Out of the corner of his eye, he saw movement. He looked in time to see an older man reach up and yank his tubes and wires out from the ceiling. Fluid and sparks rained down.

"Hey!" Bondsol screamed. "You can't do that!"

The old man didn't seem to hear the private as he plucked the tubes and wires, one by one, from his arms and chest. Greenish-gray blood dripped from the openings. Bondsol grabbed his walkie-talkie from his hip.

"I've got movement in the Sculpture Garden. Someone is alive in here. What do I do?"

"Shoot it!" his commander's voice came back.

"What? I can't shoot an unarmed man."

"Bondsol, *that's an order*."

"But why is he awake? What happened? Did I do something?"

"They must have cut the feeds," the voice mused. "Never mind! Shoot it."

Bondsol watched as the man slowly stepped out of his harness and began walking between the rows, lightly touching the other bodies as he passed. "Okay, I will."

"And you better start calling me sir, Private, or I'll have you in irons."

"Yes, sir. Sorry, sir."

To his left a woman with long black hair pulled her wires out of the ceiling. White sparks snapped as the wires fell to the floor with a loud slap. She looked up at him with glowing green eyes. Another man behind her did the same thing. And another, and another. All their eyes were glowing bright green.

How many of them are there?

All the green points of light blinked into a strange constellation, shifting in front of him. He reached for his sidearm and drew it from the holster.

"Freeze! All of you!" he shouted.

More and more movement around him. They were all waking up. The hibernating bodies were coming alive. A shower of multicolored wires and sparks was falling over the space. One by one, the Sculpture Garden was freeing itself. All the green eyes were suddenly fixed on Private Bondsol, his gun drawn, his shaky hand pointing it this way and then that way as the rows came alive before him.

"Stay back! Don't take another step!" Bondsol reached down to his walkie-talkie. "There are hundreds of them awake in here! I can't fight them all. There are too many!"

"What? What are you talking about, Private?"

"They're coming at me! They all have green glowing eyes!"

"Are you insane?" The voice on the walkie-talkie was now getting angry. "I don't like playing games!"

"I'm not *kidding*! You better send backup right now!" Bondsol tripped backward and fell as his boot heel caught on a doorstop. His walkie-talkie cracked open on impact; his gun bounced out of his hand and landed five feet to his right. He scrambled to get back onto his feet. As he rushed over to get his gun, the first body in front of him flashed with bright blue light and then morphed into a Paragon soldier, uniform, weapon, and all. Then row after row of naked bodies suddenly flashed blue and were dressed in full military uniforms. Their green eyes no longer glowing, Bondsol could not tell these zombie-like soldiers from the real ones patrolling the base above them.

He saw his chance and made a run for the door he came in through. He threw it open with both hands and sprinted up the stairs to the main floor. Behind him, the flood of awakened soldiers began pouring from the space. Topside, Bondsol turned to see the first zombie soldier push its way out onto the base. It looked up at the water tower and shot a beam of green light from its eyes. The tower supports buckled loudly as thousands of gallons of water spilled out onto the base, washing away temporary labs and buildings. The roiling water touched exposed electrical circuits as it swept up all the real Paragon soldiers who came as backup for Bondsol, kicking and thrashing in the white froth as they all were electrocuted.

The rest of the zombie soldiers quickly spread out, running to preselected positions across the base. They moved in easily, being mistaken for real soldiers, before the army knew what was happening. The zombie soldiers infiltrated the entire complex. They zapped and fought their way into the command center. The MPs fired round after round of bullets into their hordes to no avail. The zombies took charge. All their eyes lit up green at the same time, and each mouth began moving as the words echoed across the conquered facility.

"I am Kun! You are now my prisoners. Do not try to resist my army of psychic soldiers. They are indestructible."

Dr. Albion turned from the panel, hearing the words come from Paragon over the view screen. She walked over and stood behind Leviathan.

"It's the same at every base across the United States and around the world. Kun has activated every Sculpture Garden and taken control of the military. It's a matter of minutes until they march on every nation's capital and wrestle away control."

"The Chinese are surrendering right now," Belphagor announced and turned up the volume on the Chinese president giving his speech in animated Mandarin. "They had so many prisoners. They didn't stand a chance against all of them."

"That was fast!" Dr. Albion clapped and then held her hands to her face, covering a grin that stretched ear to ear.

"Russia has fallen," Mammon said and turned the eye stalks sticking out of his huge brain away from the view screen to look at the others. "It's in chaos."

Kun stood, glowing bright blue, eyes closed, in deep concentration. Rings of energy continued to flow from the amulet and pass out of the ship on their way to Earth.

"It's time for Phase Two to begin," Asmodeus said to his brothers, who turned away from their view screens to look at him. "This will ensure the Earth devolves into a feudal state. Your targets are as follows. Mammon, take a nuclear warhead and teleport to the Yushu Paraplatform rock formation in Qinghai, Western China. Opening a rift there will cleave off everything east of India and send it to the bottom of the sea, destroying South Korea, Japan, and Taiwan."

"And sinking their technology with it," Dr. Albion added. "No more Samsung or Sony!"

"Leviathan, you'll take your warhead to Leipzig, Germany. Place it as deeply as you can beneath the city capital. The crystalline basement will liquify and open up a massive sinkhole which will swallow most of Europe."

"And the United Kingdom, too, if we're lucky," Dr. Albion said happily.

"That leaves you, Belphagor. You need to go to Silicon Valley and locate the Hayward Dam. That is where your warhead is to be detonated. The entire west coast of the United States must be drowned under three hundred feet of water."

"Huzzah!" Dr. Albion cheered. "No more Apple, Twitter, or Facebook!"

Shouts and cries were still radiating from the view screens as governments worldwide succumbed to Kun and his army of psychic zombies. Mammon, Leviathan, and Belphagor stood up and began to make their way to the cargo hold of Kun's ship, where the stolen Polaris missiles were waiting for them.

"Go, my brothers. Nothing can stop us now," Asmodeus said as his brother demons hurried on their way. "And now, Elizabeth, we need to bring Kun out of his trance."

"Are you sure we should?"

"What do you mean?" Asmodeus asked.

"Well, wouldn't it be easier if there were fewer of us? I'm mean, Kun is fine as an intergalactic ambassador, but we know what a mess he made of his home planet when he was in charge there."

"Oh, Elizabeth, I love how your devious mind works. You have truly earned you place in Hades," Asmodeus said proudly as he drew Dr. Albion closer.

"We can seal off this room and vent him into space."

"And you've already planned *how* to do it."

"It's really rather simple—" Dr. Albion began to say when she was interrupted by a groaning voice.

Kun opened his eyes and lowered the twisted amulet from his head. The rings of power faded, and the stone core went dark. "Oh, my arms are killing me," he said and looked at the doctor and the demon in front of him.

"Why, Kun, we weren't expecting you back so soon," Dr. Albion said glibly, adjusting her white lab coat. "Is everything all right?"

"Of course. Those prisoners have fantastic powers that have nothing to do with my amulet. I just needed to turn them loose and let them take their revenge on the governments that did this to them."

"Well, huzzah to that!" Dr. Albion said again and held her right fist in the air.

"Have your brothers been tasked with their assignments?"

"Yes, they're just leaving. I can feel them teleporting off the ship," Asmodeus said.

"Excellent! Everything is going according to plan," Kun said as he waddled over to observe the mayhem on the view screens. "Insignificant dupes! They should have listened to me back in 1947 when I arrived. Now they will pay the price for their stupidity with their *lives*."

"What should we do with this?" Asmodeus said as he indicated the stone circle. "We don't need it anymore, do we?"

"I'd like to keep it," Dr. Albion said as she walked to Kun's side. "As a memento of all the years that those Star Children vexed me." Dr. Albion strolled over and entered the Circle. She gazed down at the pained faces and felt a wonderful satisfaction. She had finally done it. She had total control of the Star Children. She located James and gazed at his final expression, his face frozen in a scream of terror. Keira and Nga too were immortalized in their last shrieks of pain and fear. Paul and that hairy monster, Falling Star, sat trapped within the folds of marble and limestone, their faces placid as if in sleep. "I only wish it were small enough for me to wear on my wrist. What a bracelet that would make, beyond the artistry of even Louis Comfort Tiffany."

"That would be no problem," Asmodeus began with a smile. "I can shrink it to fit your delicate wrist. Anything for you, Elizabeth, my little she-devil."

"Oh, really, would you do it?" Dr. Albion asked, looking back at Asmodeus and blushing demurely.

"Of course," Asmodeus lifted his left hand and aimed his blackened fingers at the trapped souls in the Circle.

"Asmodeus!" Dr. Albion let out a small gasp. "The Serpian has gotten out! It's behind you!"

"What the—" The demon turned around as the creature rose up and threw itself over him in a thick wet blanket. Asmodeus disappeared completely beneath the squirming black flesh. The demon struggled fiercely against the gelatinous creature. The outline of his arms punching and legs kicking could be seen beneath its swallowing blackness. Finally the struggle was over. The huge lump that was Asmodeus stopped moving. The demon succumbed to the alien beast.

Kun shrieked and jumped onto the keyboard beneath the view screen and stared in fear as the huge mound of the Serpian began to gurgle and digest its prey.

Dr. Albion put the Circle between her and the oozing creature and felt in her pocket for anything she could use as a weapon.

Suddenly the Serpian split open, green digestive juices spilling out onto the floor, and Asmodeus emerged completely from its trembling flesh. The Serpian was now being absorbed into the demon's body. Bulges and veins stood out on Asmodeus's skin as the Serpian slowly moved beneath.

"Thank goodness!" Dr. Albion cried out as she looked over at Kun, who climbed down off the keyboard and stepped to the ground.

The two of them started laughing.

"How did that thing get out?" Dr. Albion asked Asmodeus. "I thought you had it locked up. Did it get out after its feeding time?"

Asmodeus said nothing. He only smiled and reached into the wet pouch at his hip, pulled out the green stone from Tenzing's collar, examined it for a moment, and then hurled it onto the floor. The emerald exploded into a shimmering cloud of rainbow-colored smoke. The colors undulated and flashed, throwing dancing shadows up the walls and onto the ceiling. As the diaphanous fumes started lifting, a pair of spindly legs could be seen beneath them, then the sleeve cuffs of a dark blue paisley smoking jacket. As the vapors finally cleared, two deep black eyes blinked open beneath a bright red fez.

"You!" Kun screamed. "Impossible!"

"Yes, dear brother. It is I, EBE, your sibling and reigning Emperor of Hjarta."

"It can't be!" Kun said, his eyes ablaze.

"And yet here I stand before you!"

Kun shouted at Asmodeus, "Seize him!"

The demon only grinned again, folded his massive black-and-white arms over his naked chest, and stood in place.

"Seize him, you fool!"

"Asmodeus!" Dr. Albion screamed. "Kun is talking to you!"

"Asmo-who?" the demon replied finally. "My name is Tenzing Bhattarai, Keira's tulpa and the sworn protector of all Star Children."

"You'll find that Asmodeus is no longer any help to you," EBE said as he approached his brother. "And what did you expect me to do after UBE and I returned to Hjarta and saw the state of it, what you had done after I left you in charge? I trusted you, my brother!"

"I took my rightful place on the throne," Kun shot back angrily. "Hjarta is mine to do with as I wish."

"And what did you do there? Hmmm? Enslave our beautiful planet *and* plunder its resources, selling them to the highest interstellar bidder! The shame you have brought upon our royal family. The Oohd name has been tarnished," EBE said and sadly shook his huge head.

"I had to watch from the sidelines all those years as you and UBE stole all the glory from me!" Kun approached EBE. "You kept me in the shadows, away from the spotlight."

"Spotlight? UBE and I have never sought tributes or glory! We ran a peaceful monarchy, and we loved and were beloved by our people," EBE said forcefully. "You really do have delusions of grandeur. And what do I find you doing now? Conquering another helpless planet. Leave Earth alone. I am warning you. Brother or not, I will stop you."

"Earth is mine now, and there's nothing you can do about it," Kun said. "Have you forgotten who is wearing the amulet, the Eye of the

Keeper?" Kun raised the twisted jewel to his forehead and aimed it at EBE. "Just try to stop me. I dare you."

"I wouldn't do that," EBE said.

"Why not? You have no power here. Even your demon can't stop me."

Dr. Albion saw her chance and sprinted from the Circle to Kun's side. "Destroy them, Kun! Make them pay for interfering!"

"With pleasure," Kun said with an evil grin. "Goodbye, brother. After I've had my way with Earth, I'll return to Hjarta to finish what I started."

EBE merely smirked at Kun.

"What? Don't you have any witty retort before I annihilate you and your friend?"

"Kun, you never were very good with our history, were you."

Kun stared blankly at his brother. "What's that supposed to mean?"

"Oh, nothing. Go ahead. Do your worst," EBE said and held up his right hand as if shielding his face from some oncoming danger.

"Do it, Kun! Get your revenge on the one who stole the throne of Hjarta away from you!" Dr. Albion hissed. "Do it now!"

Kun glanced briefly at the demon Tenzing and then EBE. He closed his eyes and focused his energy through the amulet to destroy them both. He summoned all the hurt and evil in his soul, calling up a raging torrent within him. He pushed his anger into the amulet.

Nothing.

Kun opened his eyes for a moment, stunned.

He concentrated harder and tried again.

Still nothing.

Then he opened his eyes wide, a look of complete surprise and horror on his face. He dropped the amulet from his forehead. It swung from the chain around his skinny throat. "What have you done to me?"

"What have I done? Have you forgotten the first rule of the Eye of the Keeper, dear Kun? Its power can only be used *once*. A Hjartan witch enchanted this jewel. After one use, the user becomes the next Keeper and is engulfed into the stone. You are now about to shrink away and be joined *to the amulet*."

"No!" Kun gasped as his beige flesh began to shrivel. His arms and legs receded into his body, his skin folding up and drying out like a sunbaked hide. The chain around his neck slipped over his shoulders and torso as they shrank. The amulet clanked loudly on the ceramic floor. Kun cried out in agony, thrashing his withering limbs as he dwindled down to the same size of the amulet and was fused into its glowing stone.

Dr. Albion took two steps backward, turned, and ran. Tenzing lumbered after her, his huge, powerful body overtaking her easily. He held her by the sleeve.

"No! We have to save the Twelve Heroes! Let her go," EBE shouted.

Tenzing stopped in his tracks. "What? But she's guilty! She has to face judgment for what she's done to all of us."

"That is true, Tenzing, but please help me free the old Keeper from the Circle so he will release our children. We must do this now. Someone has to stop those demons before they destroy the Earth."

"You're right!" Tenzing let go of the doctor, who grunted something rude at him and scrambled off into the darkness. "What do I need to do?"

EBE pointed to the top of the stone gate. "Place the amulet up there and it will do the rest."

Tenzing walked over and lifted the amulet. He felt the dried-up wad of skin against his palm, what was left of Kun, frozen to the jewel's surface. He stood on tiptoes and lay the amulet on top of the stone gate. Its effect was instantaneous. Tenzing backed away as the whole stone Circle began to vibrate and emit pale golden light. The marble gate snapped in two and out popped the old Gate Keeper, a very confused-looking Hjartan who looked at EBE and Tenzing with bewilderment.

"EBE, is that you?" the alien said as he rubbed his huge eyes.

"Yes, ISI. You are now free from the Circle. Many years have passed since you were imprisoned. It will take a while to get you up to speed on current events. For now, I'm still your emperor, and I will need your help bringing this ship back to our home world."

"Of course," ISI said with a bow. "By your command, Your Highness."

"Look," Tenzing said as he pointed to the Circle. A wailing wind had picked up again, and lightning flashed between the marble chairs. One by one, the stone surfaces melted away like candle wax, exposing each Star Child held beneath. James jumped up first and helped to peel the melting stone away from the others. Falling Star stood and then pulled Nga out of the dripping material. Troy and Philip both leaped from the Circle and stood watching the other Twelve Heroes freeing themselves and each other.

"EBE!" James shouted happily as he looked across the ship. He ran out of the Circle to meet his alien uncle but stopped when he saw Asmodeus. "Look out, behind you!"

EBE and Asmodeus both started laughing. "It's me, Tenzing," the demon said with a toothy grin and stepped forward. "I've been in a Serpian's body today and then I jumped into this one."

"I keep forgetting you're a tulpa and can't be killed," James said.

"He's *my* tulpa," Keira said as she and Lumen took their places next to James. "I'm going to miss you being a tabby, though."

"What happened? Where are Kun and Dr. Albion?" Lumen asked.

"It's a long story. I'll explain it all to you later, but right now I need you to listen to me," EBE said with gravity to his voice. "The Earth is in great danger, and only the Twelve Heroes can save it."

Cedric and Alexander approached EBE, followed by Nga and the rest of the Heroes.

"Listen," EBE began, "I need all of you to help."

"Tell us what to do," Lumen said.

"Before Tenzing changed bodies, I heard Asmodeus send his three demon brothers to China, Germany, and California with nuclear warheads. They are planning on destroying all the places that produce technology—"

"But that would send the planet back into the dark ages," James said.

"Precisely," EBE said and nodded sadly. "I need you to split up into teams of four and stop those demons!" EBE waved his hand in the air, and a glowing red globe appeared. "I need Alexander, Philip, Troy, and Tyler to go after Leviathan in Leipzig, Germany." As he spoke, the destination lit up on the floating globe. "Keira, Cedric, Nga, and Stephen will go to China after Mammon. Falling Star, Lumen, Paul, and James, go after Belphagor in California. I'm transmitting the coordinates of each demon's current location to you now." EBE waved his hand again, and the locations on the globe jumped into the air and were simultaneously projected into each Hero's mind. "Lumen and James," EBE said quickly, "open a portal and send the teams through."

"On it!" James said as he took up Lumen's warm hands and they opened a swirling vortex between them in midair. "Alexander, you guys go through first. We're aiming at Germany."

"There's one more thing," EBE said suddenly as he waved his right hand to get everyone's attention. "A demon's power is made up of very old magic. I'm not sure if you can beat a demon individually, but together, you should have no problem. Use your secondary powers if you have to!"

James gave EBE a thumbs-up.

"Here goes nothing," Philip said and jumped into the swirling center.

Alexander, Troy, and Tyler followed Philip as they each hurried into the vortex and were gone.

"Okay, we're aimed at China now," Lumen said. "Quickly, you guys!"

Keira kissed Cedric on the cheek and then stepped into the portal.

"Hey! Wait for me," Cedric said as he followed.

Nga turned her blue face and looked at Stephen. "Shall we?"

"Why not? We'll need all the luck I can create."

The two of them walked into the spinning portal.

"Okay, you two," James said to Paul and Falling Star. "The only fighting we'll be doing is against demons. Are you clear about that?"

"Yes," Paul said and went quickly to the vortex, but turned his head at the last minute. "Last one in is a shaggy mutt!"

"What?" Falling Star asked. "I'll give you a shaggy mutt." He ran into the vortex after Paul.

"James and Lumen, I have something else to tell you," EBE began.

"Can it wait?" Lumen asked. "I think we need to hurry. I can feel it."

"When you return, then," EBE said and bowed his head.

James and Lumen lifted the portal over their heads and let the ring fall on them and were gone.

"Now, Tenzing," EBE said, "before I forget, why don't we find out where our dear Dr. Albion has gotten to?"

"With pleasure."

DR. ALBION ran out of the turbolift as soon as the door opened. She hurried along the main hallway that led to the loading bay where the escape pods were, her expensive high heels clicking on the ceramic floor. Once inside the hangar bay, she pulled back her left sleeve and snapped a blue stone off her bracelet.

"Sorry to do this to you, Elizabeth II, but you're needed now," Dr. Albion said as she dropped the stone to the floor and crushed it beneath her heel. It suddenly sprang to life, leaking fluid all around and growing longer. Within a few seconds a life-sized, fully dressed copy of Dr. Elizabeth Albion lay before her.

"Get up!" Dr. Albion shouted at the clone. "Stand before me!"

"Yes, Elizabeth," the clone responded and slowly stood. "How can I help?"

"I'm sorry to do this to you, especially on your first day alive, but I have no other choice." Dr. Albion pulled a small blade from inside her jacket belt, grabbed the clone by the hair, and slashed its throat from ear to ear.

"No! Don't!" the clone pleaded as it tried to stop Dr. Albion with its hands. But Dr. Albion was quicker. The slit opened, and realistic-looking blood began to bubble and flow down the clone's identical white lab coat. It gasped, the last breath making a sucking noise as it inhaled through the slit. Its glassy eyes rolled back, and it slumped to the floor.

Dr. Albion threw down the blade.

"A perfect suicide," Dr. Albion said to herself. "Now I'll just leave a note."

She pulled a scrap of paper and a pen from her pocket and wrote:

"That's right. I've decided to end it all. Now that Asmodeus is gone, I have nothing to live for. You must have known that we were secret lovers all these years. But before you start to miss me, I'll tell you something. I've launched all the escape pods. You can't get off this ship. When those three demons return and find out what you've done to their brother, there will be no stopping their fury. Now that I would have liked to see."

She dropped the note next to the blade and hurried to the escape pods. She approached the keypad that controlled the first pod and set it to autolaunch. At sixty-second timer started counting down. She did the same to the other escape pods, setting them in countdown to launch. Dr. Albion opened the door to the last pod and jumped in. As the door automatically closed and sealed itself, she pulled another stone, a red one, from her bracelet and held it to her chest. What looked like a ball of aluminum foil began to unroll and cover her whole body. "Now they won't be able to see my vital signs. The pod will appear to be as empty as the first seven." She leaned over and pressed the button marked Purge.

The pod rattled and shook twice and then blasted off into the cold blackness of space.

8.

ALEXANDER LANDED with a thud at a bus stop near the Leipzig Central Train Station. He got up and dusted himself off. A tree-lined park stood behind him, and a large office building rose up across the street, casting its long shadow over him. It had a blue-and-red For Rent sign in the front window. Alexander wondered why he could read the German words the sign was written in. He looked all around and found he could read everything: street signs, billboards, even the graffiti.

That's weird, Alexander thought. *Keira would know why this happening to me, I bet. Maybe it's another power I have. I guess I've never tried it out before.* He laughed to himself and shook his head and then looked for the others.

Philip dropped out of the air in front of Alexander and landed on two feet. Troy and Tyler tumbled out of the empty space next to them and onto the ground, the two of them wrapped together like a pretzel.

"Don't just stand there," Troy said to Philip and Alexander. "Untangle us!"

Alexander grabbed Troy as Philip pulled Tyler up.

"You'd better change into human form," Tyler said to Philip, who still looked like a scaly chupacabra.

"I take offense to that!" Philip said haughtily. "I'm lovely just the way I am."

"You should change," Alexander agreed. "We're in downtown Leipzig now. It would help if you looked like an Earth person."

"Hmph!" Philip snorted and morphed into a tall blond man with a short mustache. "Satisfied?"

"Yes," Troy said and patted Philip's shoulder. "You did good."

"Is the mustache too much?"

"It's fine," Troy replied.

"What about you, Tyler?" Alexander asked.

"What about me?" Tyler replied while running his fingers through his copper-colored hair.

"Uh, hello?" Troy said. "See any other metallic people walking around?"

"Oh, will you relax," Tyler replied. "It looks like I've got a really great tan."

"Yeah, a copper-plated tan."

"What about his crazy eyes?" Tyler asked and pointed to Alexander's white-within-black swirling eyes. Alexander blinked back at him and said nothing.

"Wear these," Troy said and handed Alexander a pair of sunglasses. "But take care of them. They're Louis Vuitton."

"They're what?" Alexander asked.

"Louis Vuitton, you know," Troy said, a little flustered.

Alexander stared at him blankly.

"Oh, never mind. They're expensive. I want them back in one piece."

"They're cool," Alexander said and slipped them on. They were a little big for his face, but he didn't mind.

"How are we supposed to find this demon anyway?" Philip asked as he began to fiddle with his mustache. It itched.

"EBE didn't say. I guess there wasn't time," Tyler said. "Can any of you remote locate?"

Philip and Troy shook their heads in unison.

"Lumen can, but she's not here," Alexander added.

"If there is a demon walking around on the streets," Troy said, "I think it would be really easy to find him."

As if on cue, a loud scream came from the next block over. The four Heroes looked at each other.

"Speak of the devil," Tyler said. "I mean, *demon*."

"Let's go!" Troy shouted and dashed across the street, his image flickering in and out of focus, and then becoming three-dimensional and solid.

The others followed. There was a crowd huddled in front of the local train station. They were milling around and pointing toward the station's entrance. Troy caught sight of what they were pointing at. A nuclear missile sat on its side next to a gray-skinned creature who was slowly growing in size, his slack skin being taken up as he continued to expand and grow in height and width. Leviathan stood before them, over twenty feet tall and eight feet wide at the shoulders.

On the street next to the station, a delivery person had stopped unloading a refrigerator and stood staring straight at the enormous demon. Tyler saw his chance.

"You guys watch my back," he said as he bolted ahead of the others.

Tyler zigzagged through the crowd until he reached the delivery truck. He grabbed the refrigerator with both hands and threw it at Leviathan as the delivery person watched in stunned silence.

"Sorry," Tyler said. "I owe you one new refrigerator."

The appliance struck the demon on the side of the head and sent him tumbling backward into the station windows. An enormous crash was followed by shards of glass flying in all directions. The gathered crowd took cover behind low walls and parked cars.

Philip wasted no time. He waved his hands along his human form and changed into a gigantic minotaur as tall as the demon, except instead of a bull's head, Philip had decided on a rhino's head with a gargantuan central horn. "Tyler," Philip shouted. "You grab the warhead. I'm going to ram him when he stands up."

"Understood!" Tyler ran across the sidewalk and picked up the nuclear warhead like it was as light as a Q-Tip.

Leviathan saw what was happening and jumped to his feet, grunted loudly, black smoke pouring out his flared nostrils, and sprinted straight at Tyler. Philip dashed to meet the demon halfway into the station. They collided with the sound of a thunderclap and bounced off each other, skidding backward, making huge divots in the concrete and exposing the soil below. Leviathan got on his feet again and rushed Tyler. Tyler put down the missile and stood his ground, his huge metallic arms crossed over his massive chest. Philip got up and then leapt onto the demon's back as he passed. He wrapped his arms around the demon's neck in a stranglehold. Leviathan didn't slow down but sped up and sideswiped Tyler. He flew sideways and crashed into a brick wall, knocked unconscious. Tyler flopped into a flower bed, his limbs splayed between the yellow tulips, unmoving. Philip tightened his grip around Leviathan's throat. The demon reached back and with incredible force, removed Philip and hurled him into a nearby building site, half a block away. He crashed through the pillars and half-erected walls, sending the structure crumbling to the earth right on top of him.

"You go help Tyler," Troy said to Alexander. "I'll see if I can confuse this demon with my powers."

Alexander nodded and ran across the square to Tyler. He lifted Tyler's heavy right arm up and shook it. "Wake up! We need your help, Tyler! Wake up!"

Leviathan picked up the warhead and tucked it under his arm. He strode toward the train station, his footfalls causing the earth to tremble. He looked down at the many tunnels that led deep under the city. That's where he needed to go. Troy suddenly appeared in front of the demon and raised his hands, fingers spread. But before he could project an artificial reality into Leviathan's brain, the demon leaned down and swatted him away like a toy soldier. Troy tumbled against a mosaic at the station's entrance and slid down in a crumpled heap.

Alexander watched what was happening in horror. "Wake up, Tyler!"

A huge piece of concrete came down and shattered on Leviathan's back. He stumbled and nearly dropped the missile. The demon turned to see Philip striding toward the train station while lobbing huge chunks of concrete from the construction site. Leviathan held up his arm, shielding his face from another huge slab of concrete. This time he dropped the missile, which clanged dangerously on the ground.

Philip threw another piece of a wall at Leviathan. It shattered across the demon's chest, sending him backward away from the warhead. Philip hurried over and wrestled Leviathan into submission, flipping him over, pulling his arms back, and sitting on top of him.

Tyler looked up at Alexander from the flower bed.

"Philip needs your help!"

"I'm on it," Tyler said groggily as he stood up, ran over to Philip, and helped hold down the demon's legs.

Alexander followed him across the square. He located Troy as he was coming to, his back against the tiled wall. "They need our help!" Alexander said and pointed.

"Okay, give me a hand up."

They saw that Philip and Tyler were straining to keep the demon down. Leviathan shifted and bucked, trying to throw them off his back. Alexander quickly approached the demon's side and put his hands onto Leviathan's ribs. At once, Leviathan felt his strength being siphoned away by Alexander, as the boy began absorbing his demonic powers.

"Let me make him think everything is going according to plan," Troy said as he again raised his hands and beamed his pulsating atoms into Leviathan's brain, disrupting his senses, showing him the powerful illusion. "He'll see himself planting the bomb under the city and then it exploding."

Leviathan stopped struggling, went limp, and then began laughing as if he had just defeated a foe.

"The bomb just went off in his head," Troy explained. "He's loving it, all that destruction."

"We still need to send him back to Hell," Philip said as he released Leviathan's arms but continued to sit on him.

"How do we do that?" Tyler said. "None of us can teleport things."

"That's easy," Troy said. "He's totally in my power. I'll make him see Asmodeus. He'll tell him to come down to Hell and find him."

"But Asmodeus isn't in Hell," Alexander interjected.

"Exactly," Troy said with a grin. "That should keep Leviathan occupied for a while. He can only come back if someone summons him, and no one will know he's even down there."

Philip reached over and high-fived Troy and then Alexander and Tyler. "Great job, guys!"

"All in a day's work," Tyler said and grinned.

Troy concentrated his beam of distorting atoms on Leviathan. The demon grumbled and shook his head, but then nodded in assent.

Philip and Tyler tumbled to the ground as Leviathan evaporated in a cloud of sulfurous yellow smoke.

"Oh my God! That smells like the worst fart ever," Philip said, waving away the fumes. "It smells like one of Kun's."

The others gagged and coughed.

"I didn't need to know about Kun's farts," Tyler said. "The dirty double-crosser!"

"He makes me sick enough just thinking about him," Troy added.

"I've got a question for you all. How do we get back to the ship?" Philip asked as the air cleared and he stood up.

"Lumen could always hear my thoughts," Alexander said. "Maybe we try to communicate with her…."

I'm one step ahead of you, Lumen announced into each of their minds simultaneously. *EBE is sending a time bubble for you. Just stay where you are. And congratulations, that's one demon down and two to go.*

What about the warhead? Tyler asked.
Bring it with you. EBE will collect it along with you guys.

EBE ASKED the ship where Dr. Albion was hiding.

"I can't see her life functions right now," Sri'Yoll answered. "She's either wearing something that makes her invisible to me, she's dead, or she's not on board anymore."

Tenzing looked over at EBE. "I guess we'll have to go look for her the old-fashioned way."

"Not necessary. I'll send the crawlers and thoughtforms out to locate her," EBE said casually and then turned his attention to the monitors along the wall. "You can help, too, now that you are in control of Asmodeus's powers." EBE walked over to one of the view screens and switched it on.

"I'm not sure what he could do," Tenzing said as he looked down at the enormous muscles in his arms and his body covered with scorched and scarred flesh. "I mean, what I can do now."

"Try something," EBE suggested. "Just think about finding Dr. Albion."

"Okay," Tensing said and closed his eyes.

"Try to imagine her atomic signature."

"Her what?"

"We are all just a collection of matter at the atomic level, and each of us has a unique arrangement. Try to picture what her atomic signature looks like."

Tenzing began concentrating. In his mind's eye he saw something like a string of blinking Christmas lights. Each point flashed and changed color until they were all a dark red hue and circling each other. Then Tenzing saw that it was forming into the shape of a person, someone down on the lower deck where the escape pods are. "I see her!"

"Very good," EBE answered.

"She's lying on the floor. There's blood all around her. Her throat is cut."

"Ahh, then it's too late," EBE said.

"But, suicide?" Tenzing asked, stupefied. "What would push her to do something like that?"

"She must have known the futility of the situation and decided it would be better to end it all than have to pay for what she's done."

"She also launched all the escape pods," Tenzing said. "I saw that too."

"That's odd," EBE remarked. "What could she have been thinking?"

Tenzing felt a draft and moved his huge hands to cover his nakedness. "What should we do with her body?"

"The crawlers will collect it and bring it to us."

"What if she planted a bomb or something else on the ship before she took her life? Maybe that's why she launched the escape pods, so we couldn't get away?"

"I don't think so," EBE replied. "She was just here as an observer. Kun and the demons had all the power. We need to set everything back to normal on Earth first." EBE waved his thin hand and produced a golden whistle. He put it to his mouth and blew.

Tenzing heard the sounds of bird chirping and whales calling to each other, not the shrill metallic sound a whistle should make. He knew this must be Bodhisattva magic. A green point of light appeared before EBE. It began to grow and brighten. Before long, a huge emerald sphere sat in front of them, scintillating and blinking. It popped open like a bubble, and there stood Green Tara. She turned to face them, her robe unfurling into a collection of vines covered in pink flowers, uncoiling and flowing outward. As she walked toward them, the air was perfumed with the glorious scent of warm mimosa blossoms.

EBE and Tenzing both bowed their heads reverently to the mystic deity.

"Please rise, Your Highness and Brother Tenzing," Green Tara said.

EBE raised his head and smiled, as did Tenzing, who quickly stopped and bowed his head again and kept his eyes lowered.

"What is it you wish of me?" Green Tara asked.

"Kun and his three demon helpers have made quite a mess of the planet. Governments are disrupted, chaos reigns in the streets, fear and panic have seized the population. We need your help returning it back to normal."

"I have no power over the demons or their magic," Green Tara said and then looked kindly at Tenzing. "But I can reverse the power of that Hjartan amulet."

"And please," Tenzing interjected as he looked up, "let the prisoners of the Sculpture Gardens across the globe go free. They have done nothing wrong. They are innocent."

"Brother Tenzing," Green Tara replied, "because your heart is so pure, I will do as you have asked. All shall be as it was before the power of the amulet, except for those who were once prisoners will now be free and back with their families. No one will remember differently. But this is the only time I can do this. There are strict rules against this type of interference, but this is a special case because of the demonic influence. I will have to report to the Singularity and let them know what I've done."

Green Tara lifted her delicate hands before her and waved them once. There was a sweeping blast of perfumed air and a blinding flash of light. And then all was silent on the ship.

Green Tara was gone.

"Did it work?" Tenzing asked as he approached one of the view screens.

"Let's see," EBE said as he scrolled down to the feed from the Paragon Institute. He checked the various cameras positioned throughout the base. When he came to the Sculpture Garden, there was nothing but a large empty chamber. "It is done."

The other view screens along the wall all showed the Earth going about its business as usual, as if a horde of psychic zombies hadn't toppled every government on the globe and brought every known army to its knees. Cars stopped at traffic lights. Pedestrians crossed streets, hurrying off to work or to do their weekly shopping. Boats bobbed in all the harbors of the world. Birds flew across blue skies. The sun and moon continued to chase one another, night and day. The forgetting had happened.

Tenzing clapped his huge hands and felt a strange sensation. "Weird. It feels like I'm really part of this body, not just the latest tenant. Like I'm not getting out of here alive."

EBE considered this. He held out his hand before the large demon body, sensing it. "You're right. You have somehow fused with this flesh." EBE smiled as he picked up a new vibration. "Tenzing, something has happened to you, but I'm not sure of its nature. It may be more Bodhisattva magic. Green Tara may have done something without telling you."

"What? I wonder if that's why she called me 'brother.' She's never called me that before."

"She must have done something very good," EBE said and reconsidered this. "Maybe she granted you one of your wishes?"

"It has been my fondest dream that I could break free from the wheel of dharma and become a Bodhisattva," Tenzing said wistfully. "I have chanted and prayed for that."

"But you must understand that you may be permanently in this form, yes?"

Tenzing lifted his pointed tail and looked at it sadly. Then he rubbed his sharp horns on the top of his head and looked down at his nakedness. He blushed. "Beggars can't be choosers, I suppose. I guess I should find a robe or something to wear."

"That would be a good idea," EBE said with a slight grin.

A green spark snapped between Tenzing and EBE, startling them both. And then another spark flashed into existence in the air next to the first. And another. And another. More and more sparks snapped into life and gathered around Tenzing, dancing and glittering like emeralds. Suddenly Tenzing's flesh began to heal, the burned and charred places closing up and new skin covering them. He felt his demon horns retract into his head and his cloven hooves sprout toes and become human feet.

"Tenzing!" EBE gasped. "You're returning to your human form!"

"I am?"

"You are becoming a monk again. This must be Green Tara's doing!"

A delicate peal of laughter filled the room like the sound of little bells ringing.

As Tenzing's metamorphosis became complete, a saffron-colored robe dropped from the air onto his body and fastened itself there. With both hands, he touched his shaved head, his slender chest and old man's legs. "It's not a dream, although I can hardly believe it. I'm *me* again!"

THE DRY wind blew cold along the valley floor in Qinghai, Western China. The high altitude made the desert air thin and frigid. Mammon dragged the Polaris missile across the freezing red sand with his prehensile spinal cord while his eyes on their long stalks searched the desert landscape for a detonation point. The sun blazed down on his exposed gray matter, causing him to emit another coating of protective slime against the UV radiation. It dripped down in long strands and was absorbed by the shifting dunes.

A bright yellow lizard scurried past and quickly dove into its waiting hole beneath a large piece of granite. No clouds drifted overhead. The desert was all light and freezing temperature. Mammon spotted a recessed space beneath a towering stone outcropping. It looked like a perfect place to tuck a nuclear missile. He dragged the bomb across the red sand, making a long trail in his wake. Mammon relaxed his spine and let go. The missile slipped into the shadow fold beneath the volcanic rocks.

"I wouldn't do that if I were you," a female voice said from somewhere above the demon.

"Who's there?" Mammon asked quickly, his glowing eyes circling on their stalks, trying to see everywhere at once. "Show yourself!"

Keira dropped down from the stone ledge above and stood between the demon and the missile. She turned and put her hands on its metallic surface. In a shower of white sparks, the missile became a fiberglass kayak. "There! That should fix that."

Mammon's eyes swung around and looked at Keira. "Foolish girl! I can do that too." The demon's long spinal cord whipped Keira out of the way. She flew twenty feet through the air and landed face-first in a sand bank. Mammon wrapped his spine around the kayak, which instantly turned back into the Polaris missile.

Cedric, Nga, and Stephen landed on top of Mammon's huge brain at the same time, pushing him down into the desert floor. His eye stalks flapped wildly, trying to dislodge the three humans. His spine swung up and knocked Stephen off into the sand. Nga used her power to send the sand up over the missile, burying it deep beneath a dune. Cedric flashed into a stormy cloud and rained bowling-ball-sized hailstones down on the demon. Nga jumped from Mammon and concentrated her powers to hold him down. Her energy gripped him tightly, lashing him to the spot like a net of steel cables.

Keira pulled herself up and spit the sand out of her mouth. She wiped off her lips with the back of her hand and ran to the dune covering the missile. Cedric continued to send hail down, pummeling Mammon again and again. The demon flinched and writhed, squirting out its greasy slime onto the sand. Keira drove her hands into the dune and sent her energy deep into the earth. An impenetrable osmium shell grew around the missile. The bomb waited like a prize inside a plastic Easter egg

Mammon bucked like a bronco until he snapped Nga's mental restraints. Cedric transformed back into his human form and readied himself for the demon's next attack. Mammon thrashed his spine around and around like the blades of an industrial fan. It caught Nga in the chest and knocked her back into the stone outcropping. She hit her head with a dull thud and collapsed, unmoving, onto the sand.

"Nga!" Cedric called as Mammon's spine struck him down. He flopped around in the sand, grasping his chest in agony.

Stephen saw his chance. He stood up and pulled a silver dollar from his back pocket. He flipped it into the air with the thumb of his right hand. Keira ran up alongside him.

"What are you doing?" Keira asked.

"Watch," Stephen commanded. "Heads!" he said and aimed his left hand at Mammon, sending the bad luck directly at him.

Keira caught the coin as Mannon's spine hit the stone outcropping, bounced back, and severed both eyes from their stalks. Green blood squirted from Mammon's frontal lobes and covered the sand dunes in sticky wetness.

"I'm blind!" the demon shrieked. "You filthy humans! You've blinded me with my own spine! I can't undo that!"

"Bad luck," Stephen said.

Mammon suddenly went quiet and began to glow white, radiating a huge amount of heat. The green blood on the sand turned into steam and rose in the wind.

"We've got to help Cedric and Nga!' Keira said with alarm.

"Give me back the coin," Stephen demanded. "We need to get them behind the outcropping before Mammon does something terrible!"

"I'll grab Cedric," Keira said as she dashed over to her friend and helped him limp to safety behind the towering stone.

The coin flipped from Stephen's thumb again. It glittered in the cold air.

"Tails!"

He sent the bad luck straight at Mammon. Without waiting to see what happened, Stephen ran over and dragged Nga through the red sand and behind the outcropping. He dropped down panting next to Keira and Cedric.

"Is she okay?" Keira asked.

Stephen felt her blue neck for a pulse. It was there, but faintly.

"She's out cold, but she's alive."

"Thank God!"

Keira looked at Stephen and paused to listen. It was suddenly too quiet in the desert.

"What's that?"

"What's what?" Keira asked, pulling her red hair back.

"I can't hear anything."

"What happened?"

"I don't know," Stephen replied with a puzzled look on his unshaven face.

"One of us should take a look," Cedric suggested from where he sat holding his stomach.

"I'll do it," Keira answered.

"Be careful. This might be a trick."

"I will be."

Keira stood and walked softly over to the edge of the outcropping. She slowly leaned around the corner. Nothing was there. A twinge of fear ran down her spine.

Where is Mammon?

Keira continued to survey the surroundings.

Can he make himself invisible? She reached down and grabbed a handful of red sand. It transformed into a large rock in her hand. She threw it with all her strength to the patch of desert where Mammon had been just moments before. The rock landed in the dunes, hitting nothing.

I have a bad feeling about this.

Keira turned and headed back around the stone outcropping. As she rounded the shady side, she saw it: Stephen, Cedric and Nga were gone.

What? "Hey! Where are you guys?"

She turned back and ran out from behind the protective cover and stood in the open. The desert wind whistled faintly through the gaps in the stones. The air was freezing cold.

"Where is everyone?"

A thought occurred to her: she should check that the missile was still safe. She walked over to the sand dune it was buried beneath. Keira placed her hand on the red sand. In a shower of white sparks, it became a mound of chicken feathers and blew away in a swirl of whiteness across the high desert plain. The osmium shell was intact. It glinted silver in the bright sunlight.

I should take the shell off and see if the missile is still in there.

She put her right hand on the cold surface. It disappeared, exposing the Polaris missile. Without thinking Keira bent down and opened sequencing panel. A red LED screen blinked 00:00. She pressed the yellow button labeled ARM. The screen reset to 01:00. Keira flipped the small timer switch to the ON setting. The LED screen began counting down: 01:00—00:59—00:58.

A spray of water hit Keira's face, snapping her out of the illusion. Mammon had his spine wrapped around Stephen, Cedric, and Nga, crushing them. Cedric's hand was aimed in Keira's direction.

"He's using you as his eyes!" Cedric gasped, and then went unconscious from Mammon's tight grip.

"What!" Keira shouted, dazed by the shifting realities.

The image disappeared again, and Keira was alone in the cold, empty desert.

What just happened? Did I imagine it?

She held her hand to her forehead and tried to decipher what she had just seen.

What's happening? This place feels so real to me. It must have been a thought projection. But whose?

Keira closed her eyes and searched her consciousness, the way Lumen had taught her. It was like looking through a filing cabinet; image after image appeared and was filed away in her memory. That's when she saw it. Yellow and lizard-like, a thoughtform was creeping around in her unconscious. She hurried after it. It sped up and tried to hide in an old memory of her childhood in foster care.

No, you don't! Keira shouted after the intruder. She grabbed it by the tail and pushed it out of her mind with as much mental energy as she could summon.

Mammon clutching her friends suddenly reappeared in front of her. They were all awake now.

"Stupid girl!" the demon hissed as the stumps of his eye stalks twisted and writhed, still bleeding.

Keira noticed the Polaris missile beside her. Unseen by Mammon, she quickly leaned down and put her hand on it. The LED screen read 00:12, then 00:11. White sparks sizzled and popped as the missile transformed into a jigsaw puzzle. Keira grabbed a handful of pieces from the middle and turned them into soap bubbles, which popped immediately in the thin cold air. The other pieces she quickly sealed in an adamantium case.

"There," she said with an air of superiority. "You can't transform it back without all the pieces."

"What have you done!" Mammon shrieked and tightened the grip on the three Heroes. It looked like at any moment the demon's grip would cut them in two.

Keira ran at Mammon. As her hands hit his slimy gray matter, the huge brain shrieked in a high-pitched voice, his eye stalks twitching, and he froze into a giant ice sculpture. Keira stood back and observed her work.

Perfect. He'll remain here frozen for the rest of his days.

She ran over to her friends and snapped the ice spine off with a swift kick. Stephen, Cedric, and Nga fell to the red sand.

"That was a close call," Stephen said as he stood up gasping and brushed sand off his space suit. "I knew something else was going to happen because I blasted him with all that bad luck. I guess he couldn't see that he'd become a chunk of ice."

Cedric helped Nga up.

"Thanks, mate."

"No problem," Cedric said as he extended his hand to Keira, who squeezed it and pulled him to her.

"Were you in Mammon's illusion too?"

"Yeah, but more like were trapped outside of *your illusion* and couldn't break the spell to contact to you," Cedric replied.

"How did you get out of from Mammon's illusion?" Keira asked as she hugged Cedric and kissed his cheek.

"I'm not sure, but it felt a lot like the Hidden Mountain to me. I managed to become water, which splashed on you, and then I felt his mind clamp down on me again."

"Well done," the voice in the air said.

"EBE?" Keira asked, looking around her.

"Yes, it's me. I'm sending a time bubble to collect you all."

"How are we doing?" Nga asked.

"Leviathan has been subdued in Germany. The missile has been collected."

"Any casualties?" Stephen wondered.

"None. Not Hero nor bystander," Tenzing replied.

"Tenzing, is that you?

"Yes, it's me."

"But you sound like you again," Keira said, a little puzzled.

"That's because I *am* me again," Tenzing said. "Green Tara changed me back into my original form. Just a garden-variety, old-fashioned Buddhist monk."

"Well, I'm glad you don't sound like Asmodeus, that seven-letter word that starts with an *A* and ends with a 'hole,' anymore."

Cedric, Stephen, and Nga looked at each other, puzzled by Keira's sudden primness, and then began laughing.

"Just say the word," Nga teased. "Asshole. You don't sound like that asshole demon anymore, Tenzing."

"Well, thank you very much," Tenzing replied.

"You'll always be my favorite tulpa, rat, gorilla, tabby, demon, or monk," Keira said with a grin.

9.

FALLING STAR looked around. It was a bright day with a clear blue sky. He was standing on the top span of the Hayward Dam. There was no one around. He rubbed his eyes with his hands. Something moving off to the side caught his eye. Falling Star wandered over to the guard rail and gazed out across the glittering water in the reservoir at the long valley. It was a beautiful sight. He would have enjoyed it more had he not been sent here to stop the demon Belphagor.

The sound of boots hitting concrete came from behind him. He turned to see James, Lumen, and Paul standing together, getting their bearings.

"There's a lovely view of the valley over here," Falling Star said wistfully.

"Did you find that spider demon yet?" Lumen asked quickly.

"I only got here a few seconds before you. I thought Paul would beat me here."

"It must be your weight that pulled you down here faster," Paul said with a smirk.

"I'm not going to dignify that with a response," Falling Star replied.

"It doesn't matter who got here first," James interjected. "We need to locate Belphagor."

"I'm on it," Lumen said and closed her eyes to concentrate. "I can see him nearby. He's pulling that missile along the side of what looks like a wall. Yeah, he's close, but I can't make out where he is. It's a concrete wall around here."

"What?" Paul asked. "Duh, it must be the dam. Just look at all this concrete."

James and Falling Star were already on the other side of the dam, opposite the reservoir, staring down. At the bottom corner next to the spillway gates, a dark shape was creeping along. Seven legs were pulling the huge spider body upward, while the eighth leg dragged the missile, which had been wrapped in a thick sheet of webbing. The demon moved surprisingly quickly.

"Down there!" James said as Lumen and Paul leaned over to look.

"Can't you make him forget what he's doing, or something?" Paul asked Lumen.

"Demon minds are different from human."

"And he's demon and spider," Falling Star added. "That's weird combination."

A door opened loudly behind them. The teens looked up. A soldier came running from the outlet house on the far side of the dam. He headed straight toward the group.

"Looks like we've got company," James said.

"Hey!" the approaching soldier shouted. "This is a restricted area! How did you get up here?"

"Could you take care of this?" James asked Lumen.

"Sure," Lumen said.

She focused her mental energy and sent a disrupting thought at the soldier. She told him that he hadn't seen anyone, but the dam was having an evacuation drill. He needed to get everyone away to safety. The soldier stopped in his tracks and spun about. Off he ran in the other direction and disappeared down a long ladder that led to the ground.

"At least he'll be safe if Belphagor tries something," James said.

Paul glanced back over the edge. "Uh, you guys?"

"What is it?" Falling Star asked gruffly.

"Oh, nothing," Paul said sarcastically. "It's just that Belphagor isn't down there anymore."

"What?" Lumen rushed to the rusty railing and looked down.

Belphagor wasn't anywhere below.

"How did he get away so quickly?" James asked as he leaned over.

"Maybe because he's a demon with demon powers?" Paul answered flippantly.

"He could be anywhere now," Falling Star added.

"Really?" Paul asked. "You think so, Captain Obvious?"

Falling Star stared at Paul with a cold fire in his eyes. "If James wasn't here, I'd rip that tongue right out of your mouth!"

"Oooh, big doggy-boy is going to hurt me," Paul replied while waving his hands in the air.

"Okay, simmer down, you two," Lumen said. "We're on the same team."

"Yeah, stop acting like bratty kids," James added.

"He started it," Falling Star said and pointed at Paul.

"Would you knock it off?" Lumen asked. "We need to split up and locate Belphagor. We know he's going to try to plant that bomb on the dam somewhere."

"I agree," James said. "Falling Star and I will go down by the intake towers and look. You can take Paul and search around here."

"Sounds good," Lumen said and looked at Paul. "Come on."

Lumen and Paul walked to the dam's far edge and searched the frothing water flowing down the wide spillway.

"Let's go to the towers," James said.

Falling Star nodded and led the way, sprinting. James ran after him. Just past the outlet house, James thought he saw something coming up the auxiliary spillway, but it was just dark shapes in the moving water. Falling Star looked down the dam's other side.

"Anything?"

"No, just water," Falling Star said as he turned toward James.

"Where could he have gone?"

"Could he be *under* the water?" Falling Star asked.

"At Paragon they told me about the diving bell spider that lives in ponds in an air bubble."

"Maybe that's where he is?" Falling Star said and suddenly climbed up onto the guard rail. "I'll take a look." With that, he dove into the reservoir.

"Wait!" James shouted after him. "Be careful!"

Falling Star entered the water like a professional diver, making hardly any splash at all. The light was green filtering down from the sun above. It rippled and undulated across the bottom. The reservoir water was surprisingly clear even down below. Falling Star saw the concrete slabs and mechanisms that controlled the dam, but no sign of Belphagor. He swam down closer to the bottom by the intake vents. Nothing. His eyes searched across the depths between the shafts of flickering sunlight and shadows.

He's not down here.

Falling Star gave two great kicks and was back at the surface. He looked up at the guard rail, but James was no longer there.

LUMEN WATCHED along the spillway edge again for any sign of movement, any little clue of the whereabouts of Belphagor.

He couldn't just vanish, could he? Lumen wondered. *There's no telling what kind of powers that demon has.*

Asmodeus had been the only demon Lumen had observed, and he seemed only to be very strong and very good at tracking people down. And now he was gone and Tenzing was in his place. She turned away from the spillway to see what Paul was doing.

Paul's back was to Lumen. He gazed down at his reflection as it wrinkled and folded on the surface of the reservoir water. Paul stuck out his tongue and opened his eyes really wide. The image expanded and circled outward from itself. He turned around to see what Lumen was doing.

I don't remember her ever being so quiet, he reminded himself. *She's usually scolding one of us about some dumb thing.*

At first, Paul wasn't sure what was hanging off the guard rail behind Lumen. It looked like a long black tree limb, but it was moving. And then there was another black limb coming over the railing. "Lumen! Behind you!"

Lumen turned and saw Belphagor's evil face rising over the edge of the dam. He opened his mouth and sprayed out a blast of sticky white foam. It landed all over Lumen, knocked her down, and cemented her to the ground in a tightening cocoon. She screamed furiously and looked over at Paul. "He spits PK foam! Get back before he takes your powers away! Find James and Falling Star!"

Paul looked up in time to see a second spray of PK foam heading his way. His antennae popped out of his head as his wings spread and he was high up in the air, safely above the dam.

"Whoa, spider-dude! You almost got me," Paul said in his strange wasp voice. "That's not very nice."

"Ah, you are a yellowjacket! What a meal I'll make of you!" Belphagor hissed. "Wasp flesh is a real delicacy for spiders. But first to this tasty beauty." He climbed all the way over the guard rail, his spider limbs clicking on the concrete. He came to rest on the concrete next to Lumen. Belphagor turned his human torso and placed the missile down next to the guard rail. Then he put his two front legs on his prey and begin to lift her. "I will not only eat your flesh, blood, and bones, my dear, but also your power. It will be mine too!"

"Find James and Falling Star!" Lumen again shouted at Paul.

"I can't leave you here! He'll kill you before I can get back!"

"That doesn't matter! We have to disarm the missile!" Lumen reminded Paul.

"I don't think either of you will have time for that," Belphagor said, smiling as he flexed his mandibles. "It will detonate in less than three minutes."

"You have to hurry! Go find them!" Lumen yelled to Paul. She still wasn't sure that he wouldn't just fly back to Paragon and leave them there. That's what the Paul she knew would do.

"Yes, go away!" Belphagor said. "Leave me to eat this tender morsel in peace."

Paul buzzed up a little higher. He looked down from this vantage point for a few seconds. Then he dove like a shot and flew under the bulky spider body. He held on with his forelegs as his stinger felt for a soft spot to penetrate. The needle-sharp tip found a weak area and slipped in. Paul began stinging Belphagor, who howled in pain. The demon reached down and tried to pull Paul out from under him. Paul's wasp legs clung tighter as his venom sac pumped poison deep into Belphagor's abdomen.

The demon twisted his torso down, opened his jaws, and sprayed PK foam across the top of Paul's yellowjacket body. Paul's head suddenly became human again. And then his neck, shoulders, and arms too. His hind legs and abdomen hadn't changed; they continued to cling and pump venom into the demon. Belphagor reached down and grabbed Paul's arm. He pulled it up until he could sink his own fangs into Paul's tan skin.

Paul gasped from the pain. The wound turned red, then purple, and finally black as the spider poison began digesting Paul's human flesh. The black necrotic skin ran up to his neck and then across half his face as the digestion set in.

James blasted his full electric power at Belphagor. The force of the shock knocked Belphagor onto his side, his legs thrashing in the air, and Paul, half wasp and half human, held tightly to the spider body, his stinger still delivering its deadly liquid.

James ran over to Lumen.

"Don't touch me! It's PK foam!" she shouted.

"I'll zap it off of you," James said and held his hands over Lumen. Electric sparks filled the air as the static electricity began to peel the stiff foam off Lumen. She wiggled and broke free of the substance.

"Thanks! I can use my power again."

The loud slapping of wet bare feet approached from behind them.

Falling Star leapt full force at Belphagor, but the velocity of his body caused all three of them, Belphagor, Paul, and himself, to go up and over the guard railing and down to the concrete spillway below.

"No!" James screamed and ran over to the edge.

The struggling ball of bodies got smaller and smaller as it fell until it hit the concrete. Belphagor's abdomen exploded, spreading green spider innards out in a large sticky radius. Falling Star lay unmoving on his back, and Paul's human and wasp forms seemed to have mingled with Belphagor's.

"No!" James again screamed down at Falling Star and Paul.

James! We need to disarm the missile! Lumen's voice in his head brought James back to reality.

"I can't do it!"

"Yes, you can, James. You must!" Lumen said aloud and put her hands on James's shoulders. She looked him right in the eye. "Falling Star would have wanted you to do this. You know he would. You'll be saving millions of lives."

James's head swam with a myriad of feelings. He looked at Lumen with tear-streaming eyes. "I know."

"Go take care of it. Hurry! It's almost time for it to go off."

With all his might, James pushed his feelings deep down inside himself and ran over to the missile. He pulled the spider webbing off of it and removed the detonator cover.

The LED screen read 00:05 seconds.

Am I too late? James thought as he wrapped his body around the cold missile and tried to think what to do next. He watched the LED screen as counted down:

—00:03 seconds

—00:02 seconds

—00:01 second.

10.

CINDY KERR adjusted her black sunhat and smoothed down her black dress as she walked through the grove of young poplars deeper into the forest to find where the ceremony was being held. The sun was high above her. She wiped a tear from her eye and looked for the rest of the group. She saw the back of an eight-foot-tall brindled yeti and knew it must be Queen Chaandani.

"Excuse me, Your Highness?" Cindy asked.

Queen Chaandani turned and bent down to embrace the five-foot-two Cindy. Both wept and held each other tightly. They had only gotten to know each other recently. Queen Chaandani had seen some of Cindy's paintings at the Guggenheim, so that had been a good starting point for the two mothers to become friends.

"I never dreamed that this could happen," Queen Chaandani said tearfully. "Never, never."

"I never wanted to let him go," Cindy said. "My darling boy."

"And now we have to let both of them go at the same time."

The two hugged again and wept.

"Who's here already?" Cindy asked.

"Oh, everyone," the queen replied breathlessly. "And I mean *everyone*."

"I guess it's not every day that two young men from two very different worlds get married, is it?" Cindy asked rhetorically.

"It's a handfasting," Queen Chaandani corrected Cindy. "But it *is* like your human marriage."

"I'm just so happy for them both," Cindy said, brushing off the slight. "I can't stop crying from joy."

"Me either. They're so in love and so perfect for each other."

"I know," Cindy replied, wiped a fresh tear from her cheek, and adjusted the brim of her hat.

"And now they are both eighteen and can legally tie the knot."

"What are you two crying for?" Falling Star asked as he approached.

His mother stopped speaking midsentence and looked at how handsome her son was. His hair was radiant and neatly groomed. His handlebar mustache was curled and perky. He wore a purple sash dyed with the ink of cuttlefish from the Indian Ocean, a small strand of cowry shells around his neck, and a crown of white calla lilies. He positively shone.

"*Pyaara ladaka,*" the queen said and then, realizing Cindy was standing next to her, changed back to English. "Oh, my sweet boy! How handsome and grown-up you are!"

"You're going to make me blush, Mother. I'm already nervous enough."

"Can't a mother be proud of her son?" Queen Chaandani asked and then scooped Falling Star up in a crushing hug.

"Mother!" Falling Star moaned as he freed himself from his mother's grip. "You're messing me up."

"You look fantastic, Falling Star," Cindy agreed. "James is very lucky to have found you."

"Thank you. I'm lucky I found *him*. But I came out here to get you two. The ceremony is starting in a few minutes."

"We'll be along presently," Queen Chaandani said.

"Okay, but please hurry. Everyone one is waiting." With that, Falling Star walked back into the sacred grove and took his place with his groomspeople, his younger brothers, Rishi and Anil, in front of the redwood altar.

"Let's go take a look," the queen said and took Cindy by the hand and led her down the center aisle between the rows of chairs and guests.

Queen Chaandani tapped a strange-looking person on the shoulder. Cindy had never seen someone like this before. He wore a red fez on top of his huge head, a blue paisley smoking jacket with his spindly legs sticking out from beneath it, and he held a pipe in his right hand like an old-fashioned English gentleman. The person turned around.

"Chaandani!" EBE said with a grin on his face. They embraced with some difficulty due to their difference in height, but it was still done with grace and feeling.

"EBE, I'd like you to meet Cindy Kerr, the painter and James's mother."

"Oh yes, yes, of course. I've seen your works in so many museums. Brava!"

"Cindy, this is the Lord High Emperor of the Planet Hjarta, EBE the Magnificent."

"I'm very pleased to meet you. James has told me all about your adventures," Cindy said and extended her hand, which EBE took and held in his two small hands. "I wanted to thank you for looking after James for all these years that he was away from me—" Cindy started to say, and then fresh tears formed in the corners of her eyes. "I am eternally grateful to you. I can never repay you for your kindness."

"Oh, twaddle!" EBE said and squeezed Cindy's hand. "It is I who am thankful to you for raising such an empathetic and resourceful young man. I am truly proud to be his uncle."

"And we couldn't be happier to have you as part of our family."

"Oh, where are my manners?" EBE asked. "This is my life partner, UBE."

A second person, the same height as EBE, turned around to greet the new guests. They wore what looked like a white feather boa, only it blinked hundreds of eyes and squirmed around their slim shoulders flapping hundreds of wings. UBE had on a white silk gown hand-painted with black stripes that Cindy immediately recognized as one of the designer Gary Graham's pieces. "Oh, don't mind the Cherubim. She's still grumpy after our flight from Hjarta. Cindy Kerr, I am so happy to meet you. EBE and I love James so much. We think of him as our child too. He's such a wonderful person. We have so much to talk about," UBE said and shook Cindy's other hand that EBE wasn't holding. "I can't wait to pick your brain about the human art world."

"It would be a pleasure," Cindy said and smiled.

"EBE, we should be taking our seats now," UBE prodded. "It's going to be starting soon."

"Yes, yes, in a moment," EBE replied. "Why don't you go find them for us?"

"As you wish," UBE said, and then looked at Cindy. "We're all sitting in the same area. I saw to that with the wedding planner."

"But of course, we'll all be together. We're all family now, are we not?" Queen Chaandani asked.

"We'll have to have high tea very soon!" UBE said and waved to Cindy as they departed in search of their seats.

"I would love that!" Cindy shouted after UBE.

"I don't believe either one of you has met all of the Twelve Heroes," EBE said and looked up at Queen Chaandani and then to Cindy, who both shook their heads. "They, along with James and Falling Star, are the ones who saved this planet from a true global catastrophe."

"A catastrophe that no one will ever remember, thanks to our good friend, Green Tara," the Queen reminded EBE.

"Yes, she cast a forgetting spell over the Earth."

The sound of a microphone turning on echoed through the grove.

"Welcome friends, family, and anyone else who came all the way up here today to witness the union of Prince Tutata Tara of the Saesq'ec Clan, also known as Prince Falling Star, and James Kerr. Please take your seats. We will be beginning shortly," the voice said.

"Those introductions will have to wait, my dears," EBE said graciously. "Let's get seated."

"Yes, let's," Queen Chandani replied and led Cindy down the moss-covered aisle.

JAMES PACED around the wedding tent in his custom-made Gucci tuxedo. Alesandro Michele himself did the fitting. His mother pulled some very long strings to have it made for James. She simply wouldn't hear of her son being wed in anything but Gucci.

"You will certainly be on *People*'s best-dressed list," Cindy said. "Even if I have to see to it myself."

James also wore a matching calla lily crown, just like Falling Star's. He would be, after the wedding, another prince of the Saesq'ec realm. Lumen, one of the groomspeople, was supposed to be there already. James wanted to talk to her before he tied the knot. Actually, the other nine Heroes were the groomspeople, and they were all supposed to be here already. Only Keira and Cedric were here, and of course Falling Star.

"What's taking Lumen so long?" James asked.

"Maybe she got lost?" Keira suggested as she adjusted the spaghetti strap on her lime green dress. She wore a wreath of daffodils on her head.

"Lost?" James replied, dumbfounded. "She can pick up our thoughtforms. That should lead her right here."

"It's not like this place is on a map," Cedric added. He was wearing a matching tuxedo, except his was deep gray and not black like James's.

He had a calla lily as a boutonniere. Cedric crossed the tent to Keira's side. He kissed the nape of her neck and held her hand.

"Yeah, try telling an Uber driver to stop at the sacred grove at the end of the valley of lady slipper orchids," Lumen said as she pulled back the tent flap and entered. She wore a light gray tuxedo and a wreath of marigolds on her head. "I'm surprised any of you found this place. It is so remote!"

"You're here!" James practically shouted; he was so happy to see Lumen. "I couldn't get married without you being here. You've been beside me every step of this journey."

"Are you kidding? I wouldn't miss this for anything in the world!"

Lumen approached James and hugged him. They embraced for a few minutes silently, exchanging their deep feelings without words. James suddenly thought about Paul, and a tear came to his eye.

"I know," Lumen said. "I never thought I'd say that I miss him, either."

"I just can't believe he didn't make it," James said. "EBE thought it was because he was bitten when he was between Zetan and yellowjacket forms. He couldn't fight off the demon poison *and* survive the fall."

"And he saved me," Lumen said. "I couldn't believe it. The old Paul would have left as soon as it got a little bit tough. But this Paul wouldn't leave me, not even to get you guys. He knew Belphagor would have killed me if he'd left," Lumen said and then tried unsuccessfully to stifle a sob. James hugged her tighter and began to cry as well. Keira came to their sides, tears now streaming down her cheeks.

"Don't you start too," Cedric said to Keira. "I'm not going to be able to be the strong silent type anymore."

"Mate, there's nothing wrong with crying," Nga said as she entered the tent followed by Stephen, Philip, who was in the form of a female bodybuilder, Troy, and Tyler, each in their matching tuxedos with calla lily boutonnieres. Nga wore a light gray tuxedo like Lumen's. "Crying doesn't show that you're weak. It shows that you've had to be strong *for too long*. That's all."

"I'll take that," Cedric said and began crying too and joined the others.

"Okay, it looks like our turn, as well," Philip said and joined in with the big group hug, as did Nga, Stephen, Tyler, and Troy. They sobbed for a few moments, remembering their fallen friend, Paul. Finally, Tyler peeled off.

"That's enough of that. I thought this was supposed to be a happy day?"

"It is," James said as he wiped his cheeks. "I know Paul would be happy for me."

"I'm sure he is," Keira said. "Wherever he is now."

"I heard someone say once that grief is just love persevering," Troy said as he continued to focus his atoms to stay a physical being.

"That's beautiful," James said. "Thank you."

"We're all family now," Troy replied. "That's what family does, take care of each other."

"That's what EBE keeps saying," Philip said.

"Because it's true," Lumen interjected. "Can't you feel how we're all connected?"

Before anyone could answer, Alexander poked his head into the tent. "We're starting! You guys need to get out here. Falling Star is waiting."

Everyone stopped and stood looking at one another, unmoving.

"You heard the man," Cedric said finally. "Let's go take our places like we've been practicing all week."

The gathered Heroes began leaving the tent.

"Good luck," Keira said and kissed James's cheek. "I love you and Falling Star so much."

"I'll be right out there after you guys," James said.

"I'm so happy for you," Lumen said and hugged James again. "Falling Star is a wonderful guy."

"Thank you," James said. "Who knows, maybe you and Nga will be next to tie the knot?"

"Could be." Lumen laughed and turned to exit.

James stood alone in the center of the wedding tent. He smoothed down his lapels and looked to see if he'd scuffed his shoes.

"You aren't going to be nervous," James said aloud to himself. "You have been rehearsing this ceremony since last Friday. You know it by heart." He stopped and smiled to himself, suddenly thinking about Falling Star. They wouldn't let James see him before the wedding. That was so weird. He didn't even know what Falling Star would be wearing. "He usually doesn't wear anything at all. I don't know why this would be any different." He laughed. "I know how much he hates wearing pants, let alone underwear."

An older yeti woman with kind eyes and golden-orange hair peeked into the tent. It was Dayaaluta, the High Priestess of the Saesq'ec clan. She would be preforming the ceremony today.

"Are you ready, James?" she asked.

"As ready as I'll ever be."

"Good, let's go tie this knot." She smiled and held open the tent flap and gestured for James to follow her.

As James stepped into the sacred grove, the young aspen trees rising up all around him, he saw all the assembled people who had come to witness this happy day. His mother and Queen Chaandani were seated up front, right next to EBE, UBE, and Tenzing. They all waved at him on his way up to the altar, which was a huge redwood tree stump, six feet across, covered with a sacred linen cloth, lit candles, puka shells, and quartz crystals. Thousands of rose petals had been scattered over the altar and the rest of the handfasting area. It was like a red carpet that ran under everything. The scent was warm and intoxicating.

Falling Star stood in his purple sash and crown of lilies to the right of his younger brothers. On James's side stood all but one Hero, Paul, but a candle had been lit for him that Lumen held. The nine Heroes smiled at James as he approached.

James took a long look at Falling Star. How handsome he was in all his forest finery. His golden hair fell lightly around his broad shoulders. He was tall and as beautiful and strong as any living thing James had ever seen before. Falling Star smiled confidently at James, which made James feel a little less nervous. He didn't know that Falling Star was just as nervous as he was, maybe even a little bit more. James grinned back and looked over at his mother, who waved at him and continued to film the nuptials on her iPhone for her live Instagram feed.

Dayaaluta cleared her throat behind the altar, the signal that she was ready to begin. She looked at Falling Star and then James. Both of them nodded to her that they were ready.

She leaned toward the microphone.

"Welcome all. I welcome you from near and far. Welcome! We are here today to celebrate this happy handfasting day with Falling Star and James, and to share in their joy as they proclaim their love for one another and the life-bond they have formed together.

"For those who may not be familiar, a handfasting ceremony is only a little different from a human wedding. Both ceremonies recognize that love, like life, is dynamic. Traditionally, these vows are taken forever, because those Saesq'ec ancestors understood that true love is changeless and that every couple is unique, as is every relationship."

James heard someone begin crying behind him. It sounded like his mother, but he didn't want to look for fear that he'd start crying again. He stared straight ahead at the altar without taking his eyes off it.

"Falling Star and James have chosen to commit to one another today for the rest of their lives. We celebrate this eternal connection between their souls, no matter what physical form their love may take. Having spent time with both Falling Star and James before agreeing to officiate their handfasting, I've seen the evidence of that connection between these two souls. It's in the way James smiles when he sees Falling Star come into a room, or how he lights up at the mention of Falling Star's name. I've seen it also in the gleam in Falling Star's eye when he talks about James, or the way he holds James close when they're together. There's no denying that these two souls are connected, and that is what we've gathered to celebrate."

Dayaaluta paused dramatically.

"And here we are at this very moment, the very second which is a testament to the love that Falling Star and James share between their spirits."

She paused again and then took up James's and Falling Star's left hands. Dayaaluta looked at both young men and then had them join their left hands together in an unbreakable grasp. She placed her hands on top of their joined hands and continued.

"Falling Star and James, let there be no mistake. While the tradition of handfasting recognizes and accepts love as part of Nature, it is not to be entered into lightheartedly, because it is a sacred vow."

Another person behind James started sobbing. It sounded like UBE. James continued to look forward and focus on the altar, on the crystals arranged in a star shape there. Anything to keep his mind off the small sounds of weeping coming from behind him. He really didn't want to lose it in front of everyone.

Dayaaluta continued. "The vows you make today signify that your souls are bound eternally. You make these vows with the understanding that you are committing to be a partner to one another, and to honor the connection your souls now share. These vows are sacred, and they should not be broken, as you make them to one another in the sight of all of your loved ones as witnesses. Knowing this, Falling Star and James, is it your intent to enter into this commitment to one another?"

"It is," Falling Star and James both said in unison as they looked at each other.

"Then let us begin. Falling Star and James, I will have you make five vows to one another before me and your families and your community of loved ones. For each, I will ask Falling Star for his commitment first, then I will ask James. Once they both have affirmed their individual vows, we will move to the next one."

The High Priestess turned slightly to look directly at the yeti prince.

"Falling Star, will you share in James's pain and seek to protect him from it and ease him from it?"

"I will," Falling Star said without any hesitation.

"Now, James, will you share in Falling Star's pain and seek to protect him from it and ease him from it?

"I will," James replied.

"Then let the handfasting be so."

In a flash of light, a golden rope appeared, hanging in the air above the altar. The candles flickered, and the scent of roses wafted over the crowd. Dayaaluta wrapped the golden rope once around Falling Star and James's joined hands.

"Falling Star, will you share in James's joy, rejoice in it with him, and look for the best in him always?

"I certainly will."

"James, will you share in Falling Star's joy, rejoice in it with him, and look for the best in him always?

"You bet I will," James said happily.

"Then let the handfasting be so," Dayaaluta said as she looped the rope again over Falling Star and James's hands.

"Falling Star, will you share in James's hardships and toil, so that the two of you may grow together?

"I will."

Dayaaluta turned toward James. "James, will you share in Falling Star's hardships and toil, so that the two of you may grow together?"

"I promise," James said and rubbed his other hand down his pant leg, wiping the sweat off his palm.

"Then let the handfasting be so." Dayaaluta again wrapped the golden rope over the conjoined hands.

"Falling Star, will you share in James's dreams and work with him to fulfill them?"

"I'll do that," Falling Star replied.

"James, will you share in Falling Star's dreams and work with him to fulfill them?"

"Yes, I will."

"Then let the handfasting be so."

Another loop of golden rope went around their hands.

"Falling Star, will you honor and respect James, treating him as an equal in your bond?"

Falling Star looked over at James. "Of course I will."

"James, will you honor and respect Falling Star, treating him as an equal in this bond?"

"I will."

"Then let the handfasting be so." The final loop of golden rope wrapped their hands and tied itself off in a knot above their touching wrists.

"Now that the handfasting ceremony is complete, it's time to seal your bond with the exchange of rings. The ring has a special significance within Saesq'ec culture because it is a symbol of unbrokenness. As night follows day and moon follows sun, the sacred circle is ever unbroken. It is also a symbol of completion, as the two of you are now one."

Rishi quickly stepped up to Falling Star's side holding a silver ring in his hand. Lumen, too, came up and stood next to James, also holding a silver ring in her hand.

"Falling Star, place your ring on James's finger," Dayaaluta instructed.

Falling Star reached his right hand over and picked up the glittering ring. He guided it to James's outstretched right hand and onto the ring finger. It fit perfectly.

"James, place your ring on Falling Star's finger."

James lifted the silver ring from Lumen's hand and placed it on Falling Star's strategically shaved ring finger.

Dayaaluta nodded to both Rishi and Lumen, who returned to their places. The High Priestess smiled kindly to the couple and then raised her hands above her head.

"Falling Star and James have now proclaimed the life-bond of their souls in the sight of these witnesses, and based on the strength of that bond and the power vested in me by the Goddess Gaia and the State of California, I now pronounce you married."

Rose petals rained down on everyone. The audience stood up, clapping and cheering.

"Please seal your bond with a kiss!" Dayaaluta said to the couple.

Falling Star leaned over awkwardly and tried to meet James's lips above their bound hands.

"Oh, goodness, me!" Dayaaluta said. "The rope." She snapped her fingers and the golden rope vanished. "I almost forgot about the rope!"

Falling Star reached his arm around James's waist and drew him close for a proper kiss. Their eyes met, and then their lips, and in the next moment, their hearts were beating steadily against one another. James pulled himself closer, feeling all the love he had for Falling Star in that second, being overwhelmed by it. Falling Star held James tight as he felt him swoon a little. When the kiss finished, both were feeling giddy. They turned and watched as the first well-wishers crowded around them, full of hugs and kisses.

Falling Star took James's hand and held it.

EBE appeared behind the crowd, waving his skinny hand in the air, trying to get the couple's attention. James noticed and broke away.

EBE quickly called him over. "First, congratulations. I know you and Falling Star will be very happy together."

"Thank you. You know we—" James started to answer.

"Second, we have to get the Heroes together right now. I have one more thing to tell you all. It is very, very important."

"What about the reception?" James asked, already fearing his mother's wrath if he missed it. She spent months arranging the wedding reception. Since Queen Chaandani handled the wedding ceremony, it seemed only fair that Cindy could plan the reception.

And plan she did.

Japanese temple bells were going to be rung by thirteen Buddhist nuns while twenty-three fire eaters released live doves and Australian flying squirrels, and James's favorite singer, Anohni, would be performing. And that was just the performance part; the food would be something else entirely.

This reception could not be missed under any circumstance under penalty of death.

"I've already let your mother know that I needed to speak with you all before the reception starts. It should only take a few moments."

"Oh, thank God," James said with an incredible sigh of relief. "Okay, let's meet in the wedding tent."

"I'll gather everyone and meet you there," EBE said and went off to collect the Heroes.

James pried his way through the crowd of yetis and humans to get to Falling Star.

"What did EBE want?"

"He needs us all to meet with him before the reception," James explained.

"Let's get it over with sooner rather than later," Falling Star said. "You know your mom will kill us both if we're late."

"Don't remind me."

Falling Star and James said their thank-yous and slipped away to meet the other Heroes in the wedding tent. James lifted the tent flap and saw everyone, all the Heroes, gathered around EBE. UBE and Tenzing were there too, standing in the background.

"James, Falling Star," EBE beckoned, "come closer, gather around, all of you."

The Heroes formed a tight circle around EBE.

"You are all so dear to me," EBE began. "UBE and I love you as our own children. And I have a final gift for all you. In a way, these are all wedding gifts I have for all of you."

Philip whispered something to Troy, who smiled and then shushed him.

"When you entered the Circle of the Twelve, you didn't realize what it was going to do to you, how it would unite you and your powers into one being and one power." EBE looked around the circle at the gathered faces. "You will now find that you each have all of the powers of all the other Heroes."

There was hushed mumbling around the tent, and then Lumen spoke up.

"You mean, we each have twelve to the twelfth exponential powers, right?"

"You each possess the same amount of power that Kun had when he wielded the Eye of the Keeper."

"So, I can shoot out lightning bolts like James?" Cedric asked.

"Yes, but many more powers than that. You will only discover when you need them."

"That's unbelievable!" Keira said.

"Unbelievable, yes," EBE said. "But true. Paragon didn't know what it was doing when they created you. They thought you would only be weapons that they could command. They didn't realize that we, the Zetan race, had tricked them into creating the Twelve Heroes. You will now take your places in the Singularity."

"The what?" James asked.

"The Singularity. You are now the cosmic sentinels in charge of protecting the galaxy. Green Tara is the leader of the group."

EBE's words spread out incomprehensibly over the group. The teenagers looked at one another, not knowing what to say. What was going to happen to them?

"Didn't you wonder why Green Tara kept coming around?" EBE asked the group. "She had a vested interest, of course."

"But what happens now?" Alexander asked meekly.

"You will be divided up into groups of two and sent out into the universe on your assignments."

Lumen quickly figured out that they had an uneven number.

"But there are only eleven of us," Lumen said, and the sadness of that statement filled the air.

"It is true. We will all miss Paul, our fallen Hero," EBE replied and lowered his head for a silent moment, as did the others. "I suppose you will have to take turns being in charge of that particular region of the Horse Head Nebula. I'm not sure what else we can do about that."

"Look!" Tenzing said, pointing. "Here's someone who can help us."

A bright green bubble appeared inside the tent and began to expand, filling up a corner of the room. The bubble suddenly became translucent, and from within its glittering wall emerged the Bodhisattva, Green Tara. She stepped into the gathered circle.

"EBE invited me here on this happy day," Green Tara said and smiled at James and Falling Star. "Because there is one thing I must do before you all join me in the Singularity."

The Bodhisattva waved her hand across the group, sending out her blessings upon them. Tenzing stood smiling in the background, happily watching his friends preparing to take their places in the cosmos.

Green Tara looked over at Tenzing and beckoned him to approach.

Tenzing made a confused face and pointed to himself, as if he misunderstood the goddess's invitation. "Who, me?" he mouthed silently.

"Yes, Tenzing. Please approach."

The circle of Heroes parted to let Tenzing through.

"My dear Tenzing, it gives me great pleasure to proclaim that you are now the Twelfth Hero. I name you Keeper of the Ever-Burning Flame."

Tenzing blushed and was stunned into silence. Suddenly his whole body burst into a bright blue fire, but it had no heat at all. He looked at his burning hands.

"Please kneel before me," Green Tara requested.

Tenzing pulled up his saffron robe beneath the dancing flames and got down on both knees, lowering his head. Green Tara placed her hand over his cold-burning fire. There was a blinding flash of emerald light. As Tenzing raised his head, the gathered Heroes gasped.

A look of fear crossed Tenzing's face. His fire was out, but what else had changed?

"What is it?" he asked. "What happened?"

"You're our age," Keira said. "Tenzing, you're a teenager like us."

Tenzing felt his smooth face. He touched his ears and his neck. He held up his hands again and spread his fingers. "I'm young again!"

"From this day forth, none of you will age another moment. You shall have health and long lives," Green Tara said. "Though you are now the most powerful beings in the universe, you are not beyond death. There will be a time, in many millennia, when we again will gather you all together and choose *your* replacements, as you have now been chosen. When you arrive at your assigned galaxies, you will be met by your teachers, the members of the Singularity you will be replacing, so that they may pass their knowledge on to you before they retire."

"How come you never told us any of this before?" Nga asked.

"Because you wouldn't have believed me," EBE replied.

"But you can't just take us away from our homes, from our lives!" Tyler said, clearly angry. "We have friends and families!"

"My children," Green Tara said, "this is how it has always been. You will find that it is a small price to pay for your abilities to do good. I am not stopping you from being with your friends or families. You have the power to travel beyond the speed of light. You can go anywhere you want in the universe. Anywhere the power of good is needed to triumph over evil. You just have to be ready to heed the call for your help when it comes."

"Can we go into space without a suit?" Troy asked.

"Of course," EBE answered. "Nothing can harm you."

"And we can all fly and stuff?" Troy asked again, as he lifted his right hand and arcs of green electricity shot out.

Green Tara nodded and smiled kindly.

"This is so exciting!" Falling Star said suddenly. "But James and I will be together, right?"

"Yes," EBE said. "And Green Tara has chosen you two to be the defenders of this galaxy, so you may live here on Earth, if you so choose."

The Heroes continued to look at each other with shock and amazement.

"But we can speak more about this later," EBE said. "We have a wedding reception to attend."

"Yeah, let's get over there before my mother freaks out," James said with a little worry again in his voice.

"See you guys over there," Lumen said and took Nga's hand and left the tent, followed by Cedric and Keira, Alexander and Philip, Troy and Tyler, Stephen and Tenzing.

"Let's go," Falling Star said to James.

"You go on ahead of me," James said. "I want to ask EBE a question."

"But your mother...."

"Tell her I'll be right there."

"Okay," Falling Star said and winked at James. "It's your funeral."

"Just go!" James said, pushing the yeti out of the tent. UBE followed.

"What would you like to know?" EBE asked.

"I just wanted to say how much you mean to me. You and UBE both. To all of us," James said and loosened his bow tie.

"I can remember when we first met in that bunker beneath the Paragon Academy. How much you have grown up since then."

"It seems like a lifetime ago," James said, studying EBE's expression.

"It was," EBE continued. "You started out as a frightened little boy, and now you are one of the Singularity. You have truly proven yourself to be a Hero."

James and EBE were both silent for a moment, lost in contemplation.

"So, they really didn't know what they were doing, did they?"

"Who? Paragon?" EBE asked with a smile. "No, they certainly didn't."

"When they bioengineered us, Paragon thought they were creating a whole new world," James said and then looked deep into EBE's dark eyes. "But what they really created was a way to save the old one."

"That's correct," EBE replied. "Now, let's go to your mother's fabulous party. I've heard the hors d'oeuvres are pickled rattlesnake and cashew butter on spelt crackers."

"That sounds about right," James said. He took EBE's small hand in his, and the two of them walked out of the wedding tent and into the bright sunlight.

The End.

BENÍCIO SAW the fireball come out of the sky from the west in the direction of São Paulo and crash into his field. He had been sharpening knives when he heard the whistling sound overhead. He walked out from the mending shed and looked up. He saw it coming. The impact was thunderous. Benício ran to the place in the cornfield where the smoke was rising. A silver canister sat smoldering between the rows. He raised the knife he was carrying, just as the top of the cylinder began to unscrew and then pop open.

A strange creature with a circular head and shiny skin emerged and stood before him. He kept the knife pointed in the creature's direction. The creature put its hands on either side of its head and pulled its head off its shoulders. Benício realized that it was a person, a person in a space suit. He lowered the knife and walked closer.

The person dropped their helmet, pulled back their long white hair, and spoke.

"Qual é seu nome?" the space woman asked.

"Benício."

"Meu nome é Dr. Elizabeth Albion."

Keep reading for an excerpt from
Ghost Songs
by Andrew Demcak.

ONE

"KNOCK ONCE if you're here with us," I whispered into the still air.

"Just so we know it's you," Jennifer added firmly.

I tilted my head a little bit toward the open space in the room to listen. Jennifer uncrossed her arms expectantly. Nothing. Only the staccato clucking of the mop-top chickens Jennifer's parents kept in their manicured backyard.

It was too quiet for a late summer afternoon in Palos Verdes, California, 1982.

"Maybe he's not here anymore."

"But smell the air, Todd. It smells like the ocean. Like rubber wetsuits. Whenever Leroy is around, it always smells like that."

Suddenly, our answer came as a loud thump on the stucco wall of the guesthouse. I felt that tingle of recognition, warm and electric, down my spine. Jennifer and I both grinned at each other; our ghost was with us again.

"Leroy? Is that you?"

At once outside the tall window, the sunburned eucalyptus tree, which moments before had been as still as a chaperone, came to life, swaying back and forth, its thin leaves scratching sharply across the red-tile roof. Without missing a beat, Jennifer reached over, quickly struck a match, and lit a single white candle. I sat down cross-legged on the Persian rug. Jennifer joined me and placed the votive candle between us as she scooped her long blonde hair back behind both ears.

We glanced at each other and joined hands. Jennifer looked older than her age. I was already fourteen and a half, and Jennifer was almost fourteen. As if for the first time, I noticed that Jennifer had the most striking blue eyes. Eyes like deep water at the bottom of midsummer pools. With her body just starting to fill out, her porcelain skin, and her high cheekbones, she could easily pass for sixteen.

Easily.

We both closed our eyes and concentrated.

"Leroy, can you see both of us from where you are?"

A soft knock emanated almost immediately from the wall behind Jennifer. We opened our eyes and looked at each other.

"Okay, great! He sees us," Jennifer announced.

"Will you let us see you too, Leroy?"

The afternoon windswept dead leaves across the tiled roof. Everything was very still and silent in the room.

"Do you see him anywhere?"

"No. What are we looking for, anyway?"

"I don't know. I've read that ghosts can look like mist forming."

"Or maybe it will be a tiny light?"

"Yeah, it could be a light, I guess. I don't know. But I know that we'll know if we see him."

"Look!" Jennifer tightened her grasp on my hand. "Over there in the corner by the lamp. Is that something moving?"

The pale afternoon light inside the room made it hard to tell. I squinted at the corner. Jennifer was right; something shimmered over by the standing lamp. The air twisted. It bent and moved like waves of heat coming off summer asphalt. Something was coming into focus. Tiny white sparks glittered and swirled in midair like electrons coming together around some unseen nucleus. And then, just as suddenly as it had begun, it stopped.

"What happened?" Jennifer sighed.

"I don't know."

"Maybe he didn't have enough energy to materialize."

"That could be it. Or maybe he changed his mind for some reason."

"This always happens to us!"

I HAD known Jennifer for almost three years now. We'd met in orchestra in sixth grade at Malaga Cove Prep School, in September of 1978. On that first day, in the oak-lined rehearsal room, after I sight-read a piece of Gluck perfectly, the conductor, Dr. Gundham, assigned me to Second Flute, First Chair.

But I should have been First Flute, First chair.

Dr. Gundham knew my reputation. I was the local musical prodigy. Principal Tracy even wrote a little article about me for the *Palos Verdes News* when I was accepted as a student. He was always singling me out for attention when he needed something to talk about at school fundraisers and pep rallies. I guess he thought I raised the caliber of student.

Both Dr. Gundham and Malaga Cove Prep's music program were already highly acclaimed and accredited. Even though I played better than all the other flute players that day, Dr. Gundham wanted me to be humble about it. I was only eleven, after all, a lowly sixth grader.

I didn't complain. I had plenty of time to advance.

Dr. Gundham was a clever man.

Jennifer played clarinet, and after auditioning, got Second Clarinet, First Chair. That meant she sat directly behind me. The first song Dr. Gundham had us play that day, after settling down and tuning up, was Gershwin's "Strawberry Woman," from *Porgy and Bess*. Jennifer played the clarinet part magnificently. I could hear her distinctly. After class, while she put her clarinet's tan-colored reed away in a thin plastic case, I told her that her playing sounded beautiful. She smiled at me shyly and then introduced herself.

"I'm Jennifer van der Lipp."

"Hi, nice to meet you. Todd Williams."

"Oh, you're the one my mother was talking about. You won that Juilliard young musicians scholarship."

"Yeah. It took a lot of practice, but I did it."

"Congratulations, Todd."

"Thanks. It's so weird being at this private school. I've only been at a public school before. What's with these uniforms?"

"They're okay. You'll get used to it. I think Malaga Cove Prep wants us to stand out. You know, if we're in public. It's advertising for them."

"McPrep School."

"What?"

"Like McDonalds. Malaga Cove, you know, M-C, *Mc* Prep?"

"McPrep! You're right! We're their living billboards!"

We both laughed. We became fast friends.

We spent practically every day together after that: rehearsing Mozart, Prokofiev, or Bernstein, doing each other's homework, and reading every book on the supernatural in the Palos Verdes Public Library, where my mother, Eddie, worked as a reference librarian. But really, the orchestra kept us together. From the beginning, we both took the Music track at school. We'd even signed up for the additional PZ— Period Zero—rehearsal at 7:00 a.m., before school even started. Jennifer had natural musical ability too; she made everything she played seem effortless.

Ever since I began playing flute, music instructors and competition judges called me a musical prodigy. After all, I performed, read, and wrote music starting at the age of seven, in the second grade. Everyone referred to it as my "gift."

My mother loved it most of all. I was her shining star.

THE WHITE candle flickered and popped between Jennifer and me.

"Maybe Leroy doesn't want to materialize right now."

"We should continue asking him questions, right?"

"I think so. I mean, he's still here. I can feel it."

"Me too. And smell the air."

"Yeah. The scent of the ocean."

"What should I ask?" Jennifer said as she looked at me and then scanned the dimly lit room.

"Ask if he knows if you're getting a Sony Walkman for your birthday next week."

She grinned and shifted back and forth, leaning in closer to me.

"Okay. Leroy, if you can still hear me, please knock once if my parents bought me a Walkman for my birthday."

Jennifer and I held our breaths to hear the response, still clutching each other's hands tightly. But nothing. Just the sound of the wind, the dry branches that shifted overhead, and then the clucking chickens. A cold breeze worked its way across my face, as if someone had just passed between Jennifer and me. I could tell she felt it too. In fact, the temperature in the room felt like it just dropped twenty degrees. We both exhaled. Our breaths came out in white puffs of condensation, as if it were the dead of winter and not the middle of July. We dropped our hands, truly surprised. The candle flame danced in its oily pool.

"It's freezing cold!" Jennifer said, shivering a little bit.

"Was that you, Leroy?"

Silence.

"Are you teasing us?"

More silence.

"You're not going to spoil the birthday surprise, are you?" I asked.

"I think you're right. He doesn't want to tell us."

"It is cheating a little bit."

"Yeah, I guess he thinks so too."

"You know, we never really figured out who Leroy was before he died. Maybe he was someone's father."

"I think he was a sailor, maybe even a ship's captain."

"And that's why it always smells like salt water when he's around!" I finished Jennifer's thought. "I think he lived a long time ago, like the early 1900s."

And just then, as if on cue, the votive candle on the floor crackled loudly, the bright flame shooting upward about a foot and half into the still air, and then, just as suddenly, it went out in a blinding flash of heat and light, all by itself. Jennifer and I both shifted backward at the same time. A hush fell across the stuffy room as a hiss of gray smoke began to swirl upward between Jennifer and me, sweetening the air.

"Oh my God!" Jennifer cried out after a pause as she and I both stood up and looked at one another.

"What does that mean?"

"I don't know!"

"Has he done that before?"

"No! Not when he's at my house!" Jennifer added.

"He's never done it at mine either!"

"I'm scared."

"Me too."

"Maybe he's mad at us for asking that question?"

"Let's get out of here!"

Before I knew it, my hand was turning the smooth door handle to get outside. Jennifer pressed up closely behind me, almost pushing me down, as we hurried out of the guesthouse doorway, scattering the flock of chickens into the leaf-filtered light of the warm afternoon. We stood and panted for a few moments, hearts racing, blood rushing through our cheeks and ears. Our adrenaline flowed hard.

"That was so weird!"

"I know!"

"I wish there was someone we could tell about this."

"No one would believe us, anyway."

"I know. Even if they saw it with their own two eyes. It's too strange."

"I think it's always going to be our secret."

"Leroy was meant to be our secret."

"Yeah."

We discovered Leroy during the first séance we had in the sixth grade. I had been reading a book about spirit mediums who could contact the dead; we wanted to try it out for ourselves. Jennifer and I set up a row of candles and lit them. We took turns asking questions. The answers came suddenly from all around us as knocks and bumping sounds. One knock for *yes*, silence for *no*. I was truly surprised that we were getting any kind of response. Jennifer asked the cooperative entity what his name was. At once we both had the same thought: Leroy. That was his name. We knew it instantly. From then on he was our constant companion, his invisible hands knocking out answers on walls or moving objects around wherever we went.

I checked my calculator watch that Jennifer gave me for a birthday present. Almost five o'clock. Eddie would pick me up from Jennifer's house soon.

"I should go get my backpack," I said as we started to walk up the concrete path to the main part of Jennifer's house.

Jennifer's family oozed wealth. Her father recently became the executive vice president at a toy company that just started producing Cabbage Patch dolls, which were already, of course, a huge success. I caught a ride home every day after school with Jennifer and stayed at her house until my single mother picked me up. Even though it was still summertime, Eddie dropped me off almost every morning at Jennifer's house before she went to work at the library. She wanted me to keep practicing my flute all summer long. I kept it with me in my backpack at all times. Eddie didn't want anything to mess up my scholarship, and she let me know it every chance she got. She thought I'd practice more if I were at Jennifer's house.

Nope.

"I think Leroy is coming home with me tonight. I can kind of feel it. You know?"

"Yeah, I think you're right. He's not here anymore."

"I hope he's not still mad at us."

"Yeah, it would suck if he kept on doing weird things to us," Jennifer added.

"I'll call you later and let you know."

"Okay."

Just as Jennifer finished answering me, Eddie pulled up in her bumper sticker-encrusted Volvo station wagon: "Save the Whales," "If You Can Read This, You're Too Close!" and "Who Shot JR?" were among the fifty or so others in various states of fading, tearing, and peeling off. It always seemed to me the bumper stickers were somehow holding the whole crappy car together.

She honked her horn three long times. Patti Smith's nasal voice on the radio came wafting from the car along with a wisp of exhaled smoke. I saw that Eddie had a tightly rolled joint smoldering in her left hand, hanging out the driver's side window.

"Doesn't she see us right here? Why is she honking like that?" Jennifer asked.

I knew the answer to this question but didn't want to talk about it now with Jennifer. There would be a time when I'd have to explain my mother's bad behavior: her late nights, the strangers she'd bring home, and the next morning's rows of empty booze bottles by the dark-green trash can. I'd even caught Eddie drinking vodka at breakfast a couple of times. Someday I would tell Jennifer that particular secret. I had collected quite a few secrets in just fourteen years. Jennifer was my best friend, after all. I trusted her completely.

And someday I'd probably have to tell her everything.

ANDREW DEMCAK is an American poet and novelist, the author of five poetry collections and six Young Adult novels. His books have been featured by The American Library Association, Verse Daily, The Lambda Literary Foundation, The Best American Poetry, and Poets and Writers. He was a finalist for the prestigious Dorset Poetry Prize, the Gloria E. Anzaldúa Poetry Prize, The Crazyhorse Poetry Award, and the Louise Bogan Award for Artistic Merit and Excellence in Poetry.

His work has been nominated for the [CLMP] Firecracker Award, Pushcart Prize, Lambda Award, Thom Gunn Poetry Award, both the California and Northern California Book Award, Best of the Web, and others. He has an M. F. A. in English/Creative Writing from St. Mary's College in Moraga, CA , where he studied with Robert Hass, Brenda Hillman, Michael Palmer, Carol Snow, Frank Bidart, Gary Snyder, Charles Wright, and Sharon Olds. Andrew is also a member of the Squaw Valley Community of Writers, where he studied with Galway Kinnell, Richard Howard, Luci Tapahanso, and Lucille Clifton.

Visit Andrew at his website: www.andrewdemcak.org

ANDREW DEMCAK

A LITTLE BIT
LANGSTON

The Elusive Spark: Book One

Being different is a challenge, especially for James Kerr. He's no average teenager. James begins to channel a dead writer's poetry and then discovers he has the power to manipulate electricity. At the same time, romantic feelings for his best friend, Paul Schmitz, make him realize he's gay. But he has little time to explore the drastic changes in his life before heartbreak strikes at the hands of Paul's violent father. James is sent to The Paragon Academy, an institute specializing in juvenile paranormal research. There he meets Lumen, the mysterious daughter of a famous Korean actress. Lumen's psychic ability might just be the thing that helps James unlock the secrets of both his poems and the origins of his supernatural talents.

www.harmonyinkpress.com

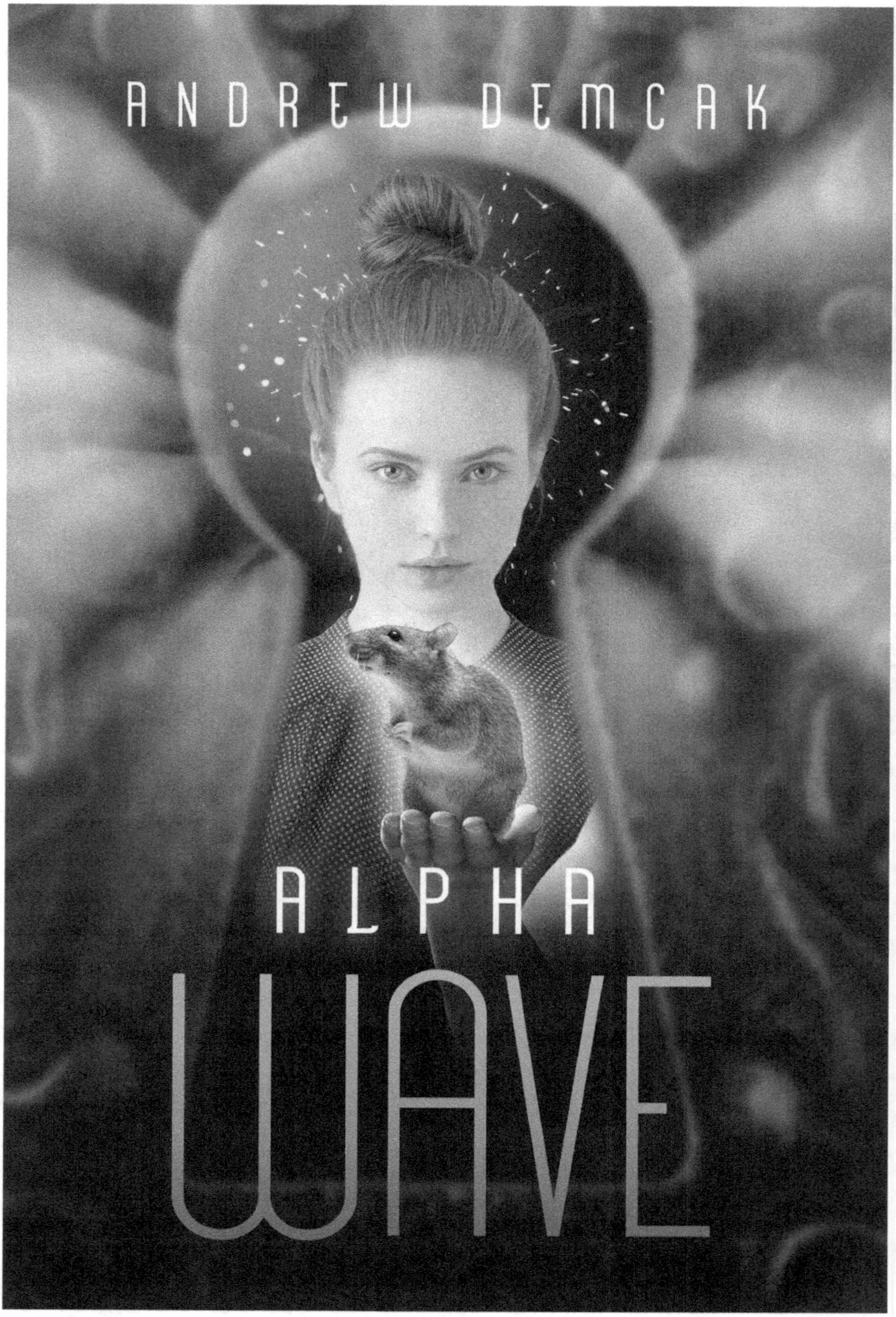
ANDREW DEMCAK
ALPHA
WAVE

The Elusive Spark: Book Two

With so many hunting her for the power she possesses, Keira Fairchild needs a friend in her corner.

On the run from the Paragon Academy and a ring of slave traders, Keira is searching for answers. Who is the mysterious alien trying to contact her in her dreams, and why is he being held captive? Keira learns she isn't alone. James, Lumen, and Paul are teens with powers like her own—and all of the teens are in danger. They've been sent by their alien father to look for Keira. The kidnapped alien needs their help, and the unscrupulous Dr. Albion has a plan to rob them of their powers and destroy them. In the battle that awaits them, standing together is their only chance.

www.harmonyinkpress.com

ANDREW DEMCAK

DARKFEATHER

The Elusive Spark: Book Three

James, Keira, Lumen, and Paul—teens with special abilities granted by their alien DNA—bonded over hardship, becoming friends and sometimes more. But now they're held in Fort Bragg and subjected to painful tests by the evil Dr. Albion, and those ties are coming loose just when they need them the most. Budding romances and family relationships are tested as each teen struggles to choose where to stand and who can be trusted. Reunions with lost family members and the possibility of love with new allies strain already tense relationships, and not every heart will survive unscathed. But the Star Children are the only ones who can command an alien spaceship needed to intercept the *Nibiru* object—an unidentified celestial mass plummeting toward the planet. If they can't work together, an unimaginable catastrophe will strike the earth, and they're the only ones who can stop it.

www.harmonyinkpress.com

GHOST SONGS

ANDREW DEMCAK

It's not easy being Todd Williams, a fourteen-and-a-half-year-old gay musical prodigy. The bullies, Bob and Ari, at his fancy private school make his life a living hell. Todd's drunken, irresponsible mother, Eddie, constantly embarrasses him and puts his artistic future in jeopardy. And now, his best friend, Jennifer, who plays clarinet with him in the orchestra, isn't speaking to him. Maybe Leroy, Todd's friendly poltergeist, knows what's going on with her. To top it off, he can no longer rely on Jennifer's help in the race to solve a puzzle that could lead to a buried treasure. Todd must learn to stand alone. He's finding out that growing up is far scarier than he ever imagined.

www.harmonyinkpress.com

FOR MORE
OF THE BEST
TEEN & NEW
ADULT FICTION

Harmony Ink

VISIT

HARMONYINKPRESS.COM

www.ingramcontent.com/pod-product-compliance
Lightning Source LLC
Chambersburg PA
CBHW051126260626
47170CB00005B/1681